STRANDED WITH MY STEPBROTHER

SUBMITTING TO MY STEPBROTHER
BOOK ONE

M. FRANCIS HASTINGS

Copyright © 2024 by M. Francis Hastings

All rights reserved.

No part of this book may be reproduced in any form or by any electronic or mechanical means, including information storage and retrieval systems, without written permission from the author, except for the use of brief quotations in a book review.

❦ Created with Vellum

For all the Amys that have believed in this book.

CONTENTS

1. Chapter 1: The Big Trip — 1
2. Chapter 2: Hank's Girl — 9
3. Chapter 3: Ass over Teakettle — 17
4. Chapter 4: Round and Round — 25
5. Chapter 5: One Big Happy — 31
6. Chapter 6: Bumping Into Each Other — 39
7. Chapter 7: Midnight Heat — 47
8. Chapter 8: Accidents Happen — 53
9. Chapter 9: Lost in the Woods — 61
10. Chapter 10: Our Little Bubble — 69
11. Chapter 11: Happy, Happy Birthday — 77
12. Chapter 12: Holy Fuck — 85
13. Chapter 13: The Bubble Bursts — 93
14. Chapter 14: From Bad to Worse — 101
15. Chapter 15: Dark Decisions — 109
16. Chapter 16: Love Me, Baby — 117
17. Chapter 17: Secrets — 123
18. Chapter 18: Now I Lay Me — 131
19. Chapter 19: Stolen Moments — 137
20. Chapter 20: The Long Road Home — 143
21. Chapter 21: Made for Walking — 151
22. Chapter 22: Go, Go Greyhound — 159
23. Chapter 23: Calling Home — 167
24. Chapter 24: Grand Marais — 175
25. Chapter 25: Whatever Happened to Bill? — 181
26. Chapter 26: Looking for Loggers — 189

Also by M. Francis Hastings — 197

CHAPTER 1: THE BIG TRIP

-Jacey-

Caleb's shoulder bumped against mine, sending a zing of attraction shooting straight to my core. The Suburban had hit another deep pothole on the disused logging road we were taking to my father's favorite fishing lake in the wilds of Canada.

I loved it there. I did not love the fact that my stepbrother was coming with us this year.

The twenty-two-year-old in question flicked a glare my way before returning to whatever he was doing on his cell phone. He'd ignored me the entire twelve-hour drive.

If he wasn't so stupidly handsome, I would have written him off as an asshole a long time ago. Right about the time of my fifteenth birthday, in fact, when I told him I had a crush on him, and he crushed me in front of everyone at my party.

I'd been celebrating my birthdays fishing and enjoying the untouched wilds of Canada every year since then. Caleb had been mercifully absent.

Until now.

"You only turn eighteen once!" my stepmother, Jeanie, said cheerfully from the front seat. It must've been the thousandth time she said it. I wasn't sure if she was trying to perk up my mood or Caleb's.

Caleb looked up and smiled softly at his mother. "You're right, Mom. Happy birthday, Jocelyn."

My eye ticked at the use of my full name. He knew I hated it, so Caleb took great delight in using it whenever he could.

"Happy birthday in two days, you mean," my father chuckled.

Caleb grunted. "Yeah, that's what I mean."

Caleb's birthday was July 9th. I knew this. I'd memorized the fact the moment his mother had told me.

My birthday was September 15th. Caleb forgot it. Every year. I'm not even sure he knew what month my birthday was in.

Jeanie frowned at her son, and I was thankful for the solidarity. My dad had more of a boys-will-be-boys attitude about it all.

Caleb shrugged and turned his attention back to his cell phone. I hated that we were seated hip-to-hip. I hated that every pothole threatened to knock me into Caleb again.

I hated the way my stomach twisted with desire every time I so much as brushed against him.

My stepbrother was an A1 hottie. He had sandy hair that was shaved up the back but left short and loose at the top. Deep sapphire eyes. A knee-melting smile.

And a body to die for.

Not only that, he was smart. Kind.

Was.

Once upon, he'd even been nice to me.

As soon as he'd realized all his good qualities had attracted the attention of a chubby fifteen-year-old with untamable black hair, he'd gone cold. Luckily, he'd also gone back to college after my birthday. I hadn't had to face him often since then.

The Suburban hit something that was more of a ravine than a pothole, and I would have landed in Caleb's lap had I not been wearing my seatbelt. As it was, I sprawled sideways across his chest.

"Oops, sorry about that, folks. No getting around that one," my father called from the front seat.

Caleb's harsh expression had me glancing down where he was looking.

My hand was on his thigh.

Worse, my hand was nearly on the front of his pants.

"Try to be more careful, honey," Jeanie sighed, rubbing my father's arm. "You almost launched Jacey out the window."

"Out MY window," Caleb added with a grimace. He gave me a very pointed look.

"What?" I asked.

"Are you planning on removing your hand someday?" Caleb replied in a low hiss.

I looked down again. Sure enough, I was still hanging onto his thigh, still half an inch from the promised land.

"Uh... uh..." I stuttered, snatching my hand back. "Sorry. Car. Pothole. Oops."

Caleb took a deep breath and raised his phone again, shaking his head at me.

"Caleb, do put that down. It's been twelve hours. There isn't even a signal out here," Jeanie admonished her son. "What could you possibly be doing?"

"Sudoku," Caleb grunted.

Jeanie turned her attention to me. "Jacey, is he really playing sudoku?"

Oh hell. Why was Jeanie putting ME in the middle of this?

"I... uh..." Curiosity got the better of me, and I glanced over at Caleb's phone.

He was not playing sudoku. In fact, he wasn't doing anything at all. Much to my surprise, except for little app icons, Caleb's phone was completely blank.

Caleb raised an eyebrow at me, challenging me to tattle on him.

Well, I wasn't going to.

"Yep. Sudoku. He's losing," I smirked.

"I suppose you could do better," Caleb said, casually handing over his phone.

This time, he'd even locked the screen so all I saw was black.

"'Anything you can do, I can do better...'" my father sang with a laugh.

Jeanie giggled and joined in. "'Sooner or later, I'm better than you.'"

My father and Jeanie were so sweet—

"—I think I'm getting a toothache," Caleb said, finishing my unspoken thought.

Masking a snicker with a cough, I swiped my thumb over Caleb's screen as though I was actually playing on his phone.

"Ugh, I would not have made that move."

When I looked up, Caleb's face was crowding mine, his breath fanning my cheek.

And there went the zing again.

"Say, do you remember that birthday where you told Caleb you were in love with him?" my father asked, glancing in the rearview mirror.

I tossed Caleb's phone at him like it was a hot potato and leaned against my own door, putting as much space between me and my stepbrother as the Suburban would allow.

"Hank," Jeanie gasped, making desperate gestures in the air.

But my father, God bless him, had about as much sensitivity as a fencepost. "That would have been so crazy. Me marrying Jeanie. You marrying Caleb."

I prayed for the next pothole to be big enough to swallow up the Suburban whole.

Jeanie dropped her head into her hands and just shook it back and forth. "It was just a silly childhood crush. They would never do anything that... distasteful. They're brother and sister now."

Right. Now I was a gross leper. And probably red as an apple, if the heat in my face was anything to go by.

I snuck a glance at Caleb, certain he must be laughing at me.

Instead, I was surprised to see his hands balled into fists as he looked out his window.

"Yeah, brother and sister. Ewww, right Jacey?" my father teased.

"Er... right," I said softly.

"Oh Hank! Look, a moose!" Jeanie cried, a bit louder than was necessary. But I think all of us, except my father, were grateful for the distraction.

"Would you look at that?" My father sighed, stopping the Suburban and leaning on the steering wheel as the large moose weaved its way through the trees. When it moved, we could see a baby moose behind it, a light brown color with little knobs on its head.

Jeanie undid her seatbelt.

My father's head snapped to her. "What are you doing?"

"Getting out to take a picture, silly!" Jeanie laughed.

Before Jeanie had the door open even an inch, my father quickly grabbed the handle and pulled it closed again. "The hell you are. That thing's a killer. Oh, it might look cute, but they're ornery fuckers, and you will either get gored or trampled to death if you bother it."

Jeanie paled, then frowned. "Hank, do you really think that's appropriate language to use in front of Jacey?"

"She'll be eighteen in two days!" my father protested.

I smiled and patted Jeanie's shoulder. "Don't worry. He said a lot worse when a fish broke the landing net last year."

"Hank!" Jeanie said, scandalized.

My father shrugged. "It was a brand-new net, and the fish was a monster. Choice words had to be said."

Jeanie rolled her eyes and looked back at us. She put a hand on Caleb's knee as the Suburban started back down the logging road. "Is everything all right, son?" she asked.

"It's great," Caleb grumbled. "It's going to be the greatest trip ever."

"Caleb," Jeanie hissed, "be more grateful. Your stepfather paid for this trip, including most of our equipment and your fishing license. The least you can do is pretend to have fun. It's Jacey's birthday."

I could hear Caleb's teeth grind against each other.

"It's going to be the greatest trip ever!" Caleb said in a more perky voice.

My father didn't catch the sarcasm. "It is, isn't it? I'm so glad you could come this year, Caleb, Jeanie. Jacey and I would get lonely all by ourselves." He made puppy eyes at Jeanie.

Jeanie giggled again and swatted his arm. "Behave! The children are with us."

Caleb snorted and looked back out his window.

While my father and stepmother were distracted, I took the opportunity to ogle Caleb's profile. Sure, I would never touch him. He'd certainly made that much clear on my fifteenth birthday. But God, he was nice to look at.

"Do I have something on my face, Jacey?" Caleb finally asked in a low tone.

I gulped. I was caught. "Uh... er..."

"Why don't you look out the window and take in the sights? It's really pretty up here," Caleb suggested.

"Right. Yes." I quickly made a point of staring out my window until I felt like my eyeballs would bleed from not blinking.

My father and Jeanie were making kissy-kissy noises at each other, and I sighed to myself. I was never going to find love like that.

I imagined I was too much like my mother. She'd split when I was five, citing a need to "find herself." Of course, I'd always suspected she left because she had a chubber of a baby who grew into a chubber of a kid, who couldn't hold her own at the various beauty pageants my mother shoved me into.

After the pageant and modeling circuit debacle, I was still trying to find myself. My mother had been whip thin and beautiful. Me? I wasn't as chubby as I had been, but I still had a fuller figure than most girls. My boobs were too big, and so were my ass and thighs. I was also liable to trip over my own feet. That was as much grace as God had given me.

I rubbed my hands over my thighs. I always wished it would wipe away some of the fat there. No matter what I did, though, they wouldn't thin down.

My father caught my eyes in the rearview mirror, and it seemed as though he was having one of his rare moments of empathy. "I love you, cupcake," he said with a smile. "Just the way you are."

"Thanks, Dad," I murmured. I looked at the candy wrapper in the seat pocket in front of me, regretting the Snickers I'd eaten an hour ago. That certainly wasn't going to help the situation.

Jeanie gave a little pout and reached back to stop my hands from chaffing my jeans. "You're perfect. You're my perfect little girl."

Caleb looked from me, to Jeanie, to my father, and back again, curiosity clouding his features. "Am I missing something?"

"Oh," my father said. "Just a little eating disorder. Every girl gets one at her age."

"Hank!" Jeanie cried, scandalized on my behalf.

My cheeks colored, and I didn't look at Caleb.

Yeah, this was definitely going to be a GREAT vacation.

CHAPTER 2: HANK'S GIRL

-CALEB-

Eating disorder?

"What, like you're anorexic?" I asked, horrified.

My stepsister curled tightly into her door. She wouldn't even look at me, and not for the usual reasons.

I raked my eyes over Jacey, trying to see what would ever have given her the idea she needed to be anorexic.

"Bulimic. And let's just drop the subject now," my mother said sharply.

Yeah, the subject should never have been opened in the first place, but Hank Collins had all the sensitivity of a post. Everything was funny. Nothing was off limits.

Mom found it charming, but it usually pissed me off. Especially when he stuck Jocelyn into uncomfortable situations, like he was doing now.

I was completely aware my stepsister had a crush on me. When she was fifteen and pouring out her heart to me, I'd be the first to admit I didn't handle it well. I was shocked.

Ever since then, though, the very thought of those mischievous green eyes and thick black hair, not to mention a body that could have been a World War II pinup, made my dick twitch. It'd become impossible to go home from college after I started thinking about her THAT way.

Hank, mercifully, moved onto another subject with Mom's direction, but the damage was done. Jocelyn looked positively miserable.

Maybe if we weren't stepbrother and stepsister, our parents weren't in the car, and Jocelyn wasn't four years younger than me, I would have taken this opportunity to show her just how beautiful her body really was. As things stood, the best I could do was hold out my phone to her.

"Wanna play sudoku?" I asked.

Our new inside joke made her laugh a little, and Jocelyn relaxed, peeling herself off the door and taking my phone so she could stare at the black screen for a while.

I held my breath when our fingers brushed and told the naughty asshole in my pants to calm the fuck down. Every Christmas and Thanksgiving, when I'd had no excuse not to come back home, it only became more uncomfortable. Jocelyn wouldn't look at me, and, God help me, I COULDN'T look at her. Not the way she just kept getting hotter.

When this trip came up and Hank wouldn't take no for an answer, privately threatening to pull the tuition payment he'd promised for my medical degree if I didn't "start getting along" with my "sister," I knew I could have made a stink. I could have gone to Mom and complained. But it'd seemed so silly at the time to cause strife in their marriage just because of one camping trip.

Then I'd laid eyes on Jocelyn, wearing jeans that were worn in all the right places and a loose T-shirt that, nevertheless, did little to hide some of her better assets. I knew from the moment Hank had taken my waterproof pack and threw it in the back of the Suburban that I should have kicked and screamed before agreeing to this trip.

Because some deep, dark devil in me knew in two days, Jocelyn was going to be legal.

It was one of the many barriers I'd thrown up between myself and my baser desires. If Jocelyn wasn't eighteen, then there was no way I would touch her. Then there was the added complication of her being my stepsister. And four years my junior.

And... and... and...

I'd stacked all the excuses up carefully, one-by-one, to try to get myself to stop having X-rated thoughts about Jocelyn. Most of the time it worked.

But then, most of the time, I didn't have a living, breathing Jocelyn sitting right next to me, holding my phone, staring into a lost abyss.

Damned right, I wanted to be her white knight.

The best I could do on that score, however, was to give her a way to zone out of the family conversations before my mother or, God forbid, Hank decided to pester her some more.

"So, how's it going at the U of M?" Hank asked, breaking the soft squabble he'd been having with my mother that had ended in more kissy-kissy noises.

Sometimes they were nauseating, but I was happy Mom had found happiness. "Still third in my class," I replied. It was more than I usually gave him, as I liked to keep that part of my life private, especially from Hank, but I figured if it kept the pressure off Jocelyn, I could make the sacrifice.

"Really? That's great!" Hank said. "And you're going to Johns Hopkins this year for your Masters or whatever the next step for doctors is?"

"Hank," Mom murmured, "we talked about this. Caleb is going NEXT year. He's taking a year off between."

"Otherwise my semester would have started two weeks ago," I added.

Hank frowned slightly, then nodded. "Oh, that's right. So, you working, then?"

"Yes. I'm going to be a part-time research assistant for a professor of mine for a year," I replied. Hank was an old-school believer in work. I respected that about him, but that did mean I knew what was coming next.

"Part-time? Why just part-time? It's not like you're doing anything," Hank grunted.

"Oh, give the boy a break, Hank. He works very hard," Mom butted in.

"I didn't say he doesn't work hard. I'm just saying—"

"We're here!" Jocelyn interrupted, dousing the coals of anger that had started simmering in my belly.

Hank looked up at a series of nondescript orange plastic ties sticking out from a pine tree and made a hard left.

We bounced off the gravel logging road and onto sloped, hard packed rock and sand. There was a truck parked to one side, a small camper to the other, and two boats tied out to the side of the landing at the edge of a mess of boulders.

Shimmer Lake, our destination, was a mere twelve feet from us, sparkling, as its name implied, in the sunlight.

Tall, skinny pine trees and some birch fell all over each other to create dark, mysterious tangles of trees all around the lake. Not that all of the lake could be seen from this one spot. According to Hank, you could portage through seven lakes just by accessing this one. The lakes we'd be fishing were Shimmer Lake, North Shimmer, and Little Shimmer.

"Okay, everybody out! We need to unload, then the menfolk need to get the boats in the water," Hank said.

We all hopped out into the crisp Canadian air. It smelled earthy, yet clean. Like wet rock and green leaves.

"I can help," Jocelyn pointed out, returning my phone.

Hank laughed and patted her on the head. "I know, cupcake, but it'll go faster if Caleb and I do it."

Jocelyn's shoulders slumped, and she went to help Jeanie unload the truck.

I stopped Hank before we joined in. "Hey," I said in a low tone, "I think she really wanted to help."

Obtuse as usual, Hank just shrugged. "She helps. She's helping right now. And every other year we've been up here, she's been the one to back the boat into the water. It'll just go faster if we do it."

I didn't see how. It wasn't as though how fast or slow the Suburban went was dependent on the gender of the person driving it.

"But I think she wants to. Does it really matter how fast we get in the water?"

Hank scoffed. "Sure does. If we set up camp by tonight, there's still good fishing to be had!"

I decided there was no use arguing any further. "Fine. Let's just get this thing unloaded."

Hank and I went back to the boat trailer and untied the canoe that was sitting flipped on top of a simple, metal fishing boat beneath. We carried it down to the water, where Jocelyn quickly tied a rope to a metal ring at the front and guided it past the rocks to sit off to the side with the other fishermen's boats, so it was out of the way.

I hadn't even seen her put on her wading boots. She'd just appeared out of nowhere.

"Jacey knows the routine," Hank chuckled, clapping me on the shoulder. "You'll learn quick."

Piles of lifejackets, two tents, four large coolers, bottled water, sleeping bags, our personal packs, rain gear, fishing gear, and what I assumed had to be a partridge in a pear tree were laid off to the side of the landing in the scraggly grass. Hank and I pulled two motors and four full gas cans out of the back of the Suburban.

Jacey had thrown on her lifejacket already, while Mom was giggling and practically falling off a boulder trying to get her feet in her wading boots.

"Don't take Mom up here much?" I observed as we carefully placed the small motor, for the canoe, and the big motor, for the boat, off to the side with the gas cans.

Hank took the carpet pieces that had been padding the gas cans and threw them back into the Suburban. "Nah. Usually, it's just me and Jacey."

"You don't think she prefers it that way?" I hazarded.

Hank's eyes flashed, and he put his hands on his hips. "You want to go down this road again?"

Damn straight I wanted to go down this road again. Jocelyn was turning eighteen, and I had a feeling Hank hadn't even asked her what she wanted. But, in the interest of peace, I grit my teeth and shook my head. "No, sir."

"That's what I thought. Now, hop up there behind the wheel and back the boat up a bit more so we can get it off the landing," Hank said.

I was almost determined to make this the worst back-up job ever seen. But I didn't want to waste more time arguing with Hank. At least once we got to camp, I could hide out in my tent and avoid him. And Jocelyn. I hoped.

The boat trailer bounced over an inconveniently placed boulder in the middle of the sandy slope to the landing, but otherwise I got the boat down there without incident.

Hank was not there to receive the boat, however. He was over giggling with Mom, helping her into her boots.

I parked the Suburban then saw Jocelyn was already undoing the ropes that held the boat to the trailer.

"Hey, is that safe?" I asked, going over to her.

Jocelyn looked at me like I'd grown a second head. "How else do you expect to get it in the water?"

"Yeah, but, won't it fall off?" I pressed.

Jocelyn gestured to the crank at the front of the boat trailer. "It'd have to try really hard."

"Ah, Jacey, good. Showing your brother the ropes," Hank said, then laughed at his little dad joke.

Mom tittered, also finding it funny.

Jocelyn looked annoyed. I saw it before she could wipe the expression away with a smile. I didn't blame her. Now her stepmother and stepbrother were intruding on time she usually spent alone with her father.

I really was going to have to try to impress this on Hank before he tried pulling this same shit next year.

"So, we just grab it and haul it in, right?" I said, going to the other side of the boat and grabbing one of the back handles.

"Sure do. It's lighter at the front. Why don't you two womenfolk grab it up there? Can't get the boat trailer in any deeper, I'm afraid.

Rocks." Hank went to the front of the boat briefly to un-crank the rope.

The boat slid back almost immediately, and I dug my tennis shoes into the dirt to stop it from falling onto the ground.

Jocelyn held the boat at the top, but Mom was basically useless, giggling over the whole process.

Hank just made kissy faces at her while he sprinted to the back of the boat and grabbed the other handle. He looked at my feet and frowned. "Well, son, you should have put your boots on."

"Huh?" I said.

"You're about to get wet." Hank gave a mighty pull.

And I ended up in the water.

CHAPTER 3: ASS OVER TEAKETTLE

-Jacey-

I tried not to laugh at Caleb when he went thigh deep into the water. I really tried.

But when he also managed to trip over a large rock and land right on his ass, I couldn't stop a hearty guffaw from escaping me. It wasn't ladylike in the slightest. But it was honest.

Luckily, Jeanie and my father were also laughing.

"Gonna be a cold trip to camp for you," my father chuckled, holding out a hand to Caleb to haul him back to his feet.

"I'll go change," Caleb muttered and dug his tennis shoes into the loose sand beneath him, coming out of the water with a sucking sound at his feet.

"Don't forget your boots this time!" my father called.

It was September in Ontario, and we were several hours north of Thunder Bay. Today, it was about seventy degrees, but that wouldn't mean a thing once we were out on the open water. Caleb would be freezing in wind-whipped, wet clothes.

Caleb had a few choice words for my father that he said under his breath as he passed me, but I certainly wasn't going to tell Dad. He was so angry, in fact, that he grabbed my father's pack instead of his own as he marched off into the woods.

I could hardly blame him. They were both blue.

Jeanie didn't notice, but my father had a knowing expression on his face and was chortling to himself.

I sighed, and while Jeanie and my father began loading up the boat and the canoe with our gear, I grabbed Caleb's pack and went to find him.

"Caleb!" I called, walking carefully over thin fallen birch trees and through knee-high green weeds. "Caleb, you took the wrong—"

Whatever else I'd been about to say lodged itself in my throat. Caleb Killeen, the unwelcome rogue of every wet dream I'd ever had, was standing, naked, between two thin pines.

I saw him in profile, which meant I got an eyeful of not only a hard, toned ass, but also toned abs, a strong back, wide shoulders, and muscular arms and legs. I could even see his... well... IT. He seemed rather well-endowed in that department, but then, I'd never seen one up close and personal. All I had to go on was a secret dare visit my friends and I took to Sex World once.

It took me a good two minutes to realize Caleb had seen me. He folded his arms over his chest and turned to face me, still in nothing but his birthday suit.

"Need something, Jocelyn?" Caleb asked me.

Oh, did I. Heat pooled between my legs as I tried very, very hard to raise my eyes somewhere above his waist. "I..."

"You know, our parents aren't more than ten yards away. You really want to do this here and now?" Caleb went on, his voice sultry in a way I'd never heard it before.

"Do... what?" I asked, finally managing to peel my eyes off his pecs and meet his gaze.

Caleb gave me a slow smile. "Let's not play games, Jocelyn. You came out here hoping for something. Did you get your fill, or were you hoping for... more?"

I didn't know my jaw was hanging open until I had to use it to form more words. "Dad's... pack... not... yours..." I stuttered.

Apparently, Caleb hadn't been expecting that. "Pardon?"

I slung Caleb's pack off my shoulder and held it at arm's length, though my arm was shaking. I told myself it was because the pack was heavy.

"You... you have... Dad's... pack," I tried again, squeezing my eyes closed.

Caleb was silent for a moment. Then there was a rummaging sound. "Shit!"

I didn't move. I didn't dare open my eyes. It didn't matter, anyway. Caleb's naked body would forever be seared to the back of my eyelids.

More rummaging and a few swear words later, and a wet splat-splat sound began approaching me.

Warmth radiated from Caleb's body and his breath fanned the wisps of hair that had escaped my braid. His strong hand covered mine and pried his pack loose from my fingers.

"You can open your eyes, Jocelyn. I'm not naked," Caleb said quietly.

I peeked one eye open, then the other. "S-Sorry. Really was just trying to help."

"I know," Caleb replied. "And I'm sorry. I thought you were here for... something else."

As his blue eyes bored into my green ones, I felt my stomach do a flip-flop. "Like what?" I whispered.

Caleb's eyes dropped to my lips, his hand reaching out to play with the end of my braid. "Go back to the landing."

His voice was gravelly. I'd have called it tortured, if I had to guess, but no man had ever spoken to me with that tone before. "But—"

"Go back to the landing, Jocelyn!" Caleb barked, dropping my braid as though it had burned him.

I stumbled over my own boots, backpedaling away from him. "Sorry!" I said. "Sorry, sorry!"

Even as I made my hasty retreat, I turned around and saw Caleb walking back over to my father's pack with his slung over his shoulder. He was wearing his wet boxers from his tumble into the lake, and the gray cotton left nothing to the imagination.

When I got back to the landing, I was flustered and confused as hell. What exactly had Caleb been trying to do? Why did he think I was there in the first place? What the hell was going on?

"Sunburnt already?" Jeanie clucked when she saw me coming out of the brush. She reached into a bag she'd kept with her in the car and took out some sunscreen. "You can never be too careful." Jeanie popped open the top and began dabbing some on my face.

"It's fine. I just wanted to give Caleb his bag so he could get changed," I said in a rush. Though I did let her mother-hen me a little more, since it made her happy.

"You brought him his bag?" my father asked, sounding as though I'd canceled Christmas.

I frowned at him around Jeanie's shoulder. "Of course I did! Did you want him walking back here naked?"

"He wouldn't have walked back here naked. Just a little less GQ," my father huffed.

Jeanie finished rubbing the sunscreen into my skin. "Hank Collins, did you send my son off into the woods with your clothes? He won't be able to fit into them!" She patted my arm. "You're such a love, Jacey, taking care of your brother that way."

"Taking care of your brother what way?" Caleb asked, sauntering back toward us as though I hadn't just seen him naked and he hadn't... hadn't...

Hadn't what? Thrown himself at me? I doubted that.

"Well, it seems Hank here was hoping you'd come back here in some ratty camo pants and a 'Gone Fishin'' T-shirt," Jeanie explained, her eyes still admonishing her husband. "Forgetting, of course, that his pants will fall off you, and his shirt will be like Saran Wrap."

"Yeah," Caleb agreed. "If it weren't for Jocelyn, I might have ended up exposing myself to innocent young eyes."

I took several deep breaths to stop myself from going even more red. I was pretty sure Jeanie had eucalyptus in that bag, too.

"I suppose," my father grumped. "But it would have been damn funny."

"I think you and I have different definitions—" Caleb began.

"Why don't we finish packing up the boats, yes?" Jeanie cut in quickly before the two men could fight.

For some reason, my father always seemed to rub Caleb the wrong way. I helped Jeanie keep the peace by trotting over to grab the boxed kerosene lanterns and hurrying to the boats. Jeanie grabbed her go-bag with all the remedies in it and a box of rope.

Caleb and my father eyeballed each other for a moment then went to load the coolers and gas cans before we started layering tents and packs and other gear over them. My father got the motors ready on the boat and the canoe while Caleb went and parked the Suburban in a clearing just off the logging road.

"Boy needs to get a sense of humor," my father complained to Jeanie.

"He's just under a lot of pressure, honey bear," Jeanie replied. "I'm sure he'll come around. This will be a fantastic vacation."

Once the boats were packed, I hopped in the back of the canoe, assuming I'd be running the motor.

"No, Jacey, I'm going to need you up front to direct Caleb," my father said. "Let the menfolk take the boats through."

"But... Dad, there are rapids. Has Caleb ever even run a motor before?" I asked.

My father frowned at me. "I don't remember ever letting you shoot the rapids. Caleb's a grown man. He'll figure it out."

I looked helplessly at Jeanie, but she only shrugged. It seemed I was outnumbered.

Or maybe I wasn't. "I don't see any reason why Jocelyn can't run the motor," Caleb said.

"You gonna tell me now that you've never run a motor before?" my father scoffed.

Caleb's nostrils flared. "I have. On a speedboat."

"This'll be easy by comparison. Come on, hop on. Jacey will push you off," my father ordered.

"It's okay," I told Caleb quickly. "Just do as he says." I didn't want there to be a fight. Not right at the beginning of our trip.

"It's really not okay." Caleb took a step toward my father's boat.

I put a hand on one corded arm. "Please."

Caleb looked down at me for a long time. Then he turned and crawled into the canoe, making his way back to the motor that had been attached to the flat end.

I untied the canoe and shoved us off. "You can pull the string now," I said when I determined we were far enough away from shore. "The motor blade shouldn't hit anything this far out."

Caleb nodded and began tugging at the cord.

My father had shoved his boat off himself, with Jeanie sitting pretty as a princess and giggling in the middle. He kissed his wife as he basically crawled right over her to get to the motor. He got their motor going in one swift pull, then sat back to gloat while Caleb had to pull several times and still couldn't get ours going.

"He's enjoying this," Caleb grunted so only I could hear.

I sighed. "Probably. Okay, Caleb, this could be one of three things. One, you might not be giving the rope a strong enough pull. Two, the engine could be flooded. Or, three, there isn't enough gas squeezed in there to get it to turn over. Try squeezing that bulb two or three times."

Caleb raked his hand angrily over his hair and did as I said, squeezing the bulb. He pulled the rope again. This time, the engine turned over, and the motor buzzed happily.

"He should have let you drive the boat," Caleb gritted out.

"It's okay," I said again. "Great learning opportunity for you."

My father laughed and clapped his hands. "Great job, Caleb! See, Jacey, I told you he'd get the hang of it. Now, follow me! When I go to the left or right, you go to the left or right. When I slow down, you slow down. Got it? There are rocks like giants' teeth all over this lake, but I've been up here often enough to know where they are."

"Fine," Caleb said.

My father shook his head and muttered something to Jeanie, who threw a pleading look our way when my father wasn't looking.

"Let's just try to make this work for your mom's sake, all right?" I shouted over the sound of our motor as Caleb engaged the throttle and had us speeding across the lake after my father.

Caleb shook his head at me. "Gosh, Jocelyn, you'd think it was our parents' honeymoon and not your eighteenth birthday. I don't know why you put up with his shit."

I winced and bowed my head, pulling the brim of my baseball cap lower over my eyes.

"Shit," Caleb said, just loud enough to be heard over the motor. "Shit, Jocelyn, I'm sorry. I'm doing everything wrong. It's not your fault your dad can be a huge prick."

"How about you just concentrate on not hitting that big rock there, and we'll just talk if we have to," I replied before lapsing into silence, keeping my head down so Caleb could see in front of him.

To his credit, Caleb left me alone after that. My father, doing a little showboating with his more powerful motor, stayed impossibly far ahead of us, stopping here and there and waiting for us to catch up.

I could almost see the steam coming out of Caleb's ears.

"Wanted to make sure you didn't get lost back there," my father chuckled as he bobbed about ten yards away from the rapids.

"Jocelyn is a great navigator," Caleb said. "We didn't have any problems. Even though you made it a little hard to follow you, seeing as you gave us the smaller motor."

I sat up and dug my nails into Caleb's knee.

My father's expression soured. "Boy, you take the fun out of everything."

Caleb ignored my nails. "Well, you're the one who kept saying how dangerous this lake is, and then went buzzing off two miles ahead of u—"

"So, Dad, why don't you explain to Caleb about the rapids?" I interrupted.

Jeanie gave me a grateful look.

My father grumbled a bit, then squared his shoulders and launched into an explanation of the rapids. "You see where that rock is right there? With the water running over it? You aim straight for it. Also, unlock the motor so it bounces. If the motor's locked, you might lose a propeller, and then you're screwed."

"Fine," Caleb replied through gritted teeth.

"We're lucky. Water's high enough that we don't have to pull the boats through; we can just motor through," my father continued. "Jacey, you take a paddle and push off the rocks if you need to."

I already had a paddle in my hand.

"Now, follow me!" My father carefully navigated his boat against and through the rapids.

It was a good thing they went through without incident because it didn't look as though Jeanie would know what to do with a paddle.

I looked back at Caleb. "Our turn."

"Joy." Caleb took a deep breath and went the way my father had gone—only a little too far to the right.

"Oh crap!" I yelped as the water caught us and sent us spinning sideways.

CHAPTER 4: ROUND AND ROUND

-Caleb-

"Fuck!" I said as I tried to right our course. But the canoe just kept snaking back and forth against the water, out of my control.

I could hear Hank shouting off in the distance, but I couldn't hear what he was saying over the roar of the water and the sputtering of the motor.

We were headed sideways, no matter what I did, straight for a rock.

Then Jocelyn knelt up at the front of the canoe and pushed off the rock with her paddle, hard.

She righted the canoe just enough for me to get things back under control. I powered the rest of the way through the rapids with Jocelyn on alert at the front for more rocks.

My pulse slowly stuttered back to normal. By the time we pulled up next to Hank and Mom, I was ready to murder the man.

"I told you to back out and try again," Hank said, exasperated. "Jeez, couldn't you hear me? You could have flipped the canoe!"

A dark spew of words, most of them colorful, bubbled up inside me to tell the bastard off once and for all, but I felt Jocelyn's nails dig into my knee again.

"We got through okay, Dad," she pointed out. "See? Everybody's in one piece."

Hank looked about ready to give me a telling off, but Mom grabbed his arm. Between the two women holding us back, we ended up having a glaring contest instead of spewing the vitriol that was boiling between us.

"Try to follow instructions next time," was Hank's final word on the subject before turning back to his motor and starting to navigate his boat ahead.

I growled in my throat, but Jocelyn's nails dug in harder, and I forced myself to count backward from ten. Or rather, eighteen. Because this was Jocelyn's eighteenth birthday celebration, and I shouldn't be the one to ruin it by getting into a knock down, drag out with Hank.

"You should have been the one doing this," I grumbled to Jocelyn as I turned the canoe in the direction Hank had gone.

Jocelyn ducked her head. "Sorry. Dad didn't want me to, but I guess I messed up..."

I wanted to tip her chin up, touch that smooth skin with reassurance, but instead I just stared at her. "That wasn't a critique, Jocelyn. That was the truth. Your father was wrong."

"It's a critique of him," Jocelyn said, rubbing her thumb over her nails, a nervous habit she'd had ever since I'd met her.

"He deserves critiquing," I assured her, but that only seemed to make her more agitated. I sighed and patted her knee. "Never mind. I'll leave it, for now."

Jocelyn nodded and crawled back to the front of the canoe.

I closed my eyes a moment, trying not to ogle my stepsister's perfect ass as she moved. Once she was settled, I opened the motor up full throttle and tried to catch up with Hank, but he was miles ahead of us again.

The silence that lapsed between us brought me back to our moment in the woods. I'd been thinking about it, and kicking myself, since the very second she turned her back and fled from me. I'd been a thousand kinds of stupid, misreading the entire situation. Without the danger of this boat ride to distract us, things were going to be awkward.

Still, I couldn't forget the way her heated eyes trailed up my body. The feel of her soft, thick hair between my fingers.

I still wondered what it would be like to kiss those plump, perfect, pink lips.

My jeans started to get very uncomfortable, and I grimaced. If it hadn't been for the lifejacket she'd been wearing, I'd have probably openly appreciated her breasts as well. They were big, and bouncy, and every man's wet dream.

Hank took a sharp left, and I shook myself. I really had to stop fantasizing about Jocelyn. Even away at college, I'd wake up with my dick in my hand, imagining her underneath me. Fuck, I knew she'd taste so good.

"Here we are, home sweet home!" Hank called as he cut his motor, tilted it up, and slid gracefully up to a narrow, sandy beach on one side of a peninsula.

I aimed the canoe at the beach and did the same, praying that, this time, I didn't make a jackass of myself. We hit the sand smoothly, and Jocelyn jumped right out and pulled the canoe up further, then secured it to a low-hanging branch with the lead rope.

Mom giggled while Hank maneuvered around her again to get the boat pulled halfway up on shore, tying his off as well. Then he gallantly held out his hand and helped Mom get out of the boat.

If Jocelyn was going to be my partner for this trip, well, I was glad. She knew the score. Mom seemed happy to be utterly useless.

I froze and looked at Jocelyn, who was grabbing gear and marching up a small incline to offload it somewhere I couldn't see through the trees. Were we supposed to be partners this trip? Was I going to be stuck in a boat with her for ten days?!

My balls were not going to be blue. They were going to turn black and fall off.

"Caleb, help your sister," Hank chuckled as he kissed Mom on the shoreline.

A nasty retort about him not doing jack shit just about bubbled out of my mouth, but then Jocelyn grabbed two sleeping bags, and I got to watch her ass wiggle as she deftly dodged a tree root to go back up the path. It was enough of a distraction to calm me down.

I jumped out of the canoe and started grabbing cots and tents, the loosely tied stuff on top of our heavier gear. Once we'd cleared that, Jocelyn reached for one handle of a cooler, and I reached for the other.

"Jacey, why don't you help your stepmother over here with the pillows and seat cushions? Caleb and I can get the coolers," Hank said.

Jocelyn hunched a little, but nodded and went to help Mom. I balled both fists around the cooler handle to stop myself from decking Hank. It was clear father and daughter had developed a routine that he was breaking for some reason. Maybe to show off what a good father he was to Mom.

In any case, he was treating Jocelyn like an infant, and it was pissing me off.

"Lift with your knees," Hank grunted as he heaved up his end of the cooler.

I lifted mine, and we walked the cooler up the incline and into the trees.

Our campsite, it turned out, was a real fishermen's hideaway. There was a nice, big, flat area with a makeshift picnic table of sorts made of stumps, branches, and boards to one side. Other, smaller flat areas dotted a trail that disappeared further up the hill.

"We've even got a pot here," Hank said proudly. When we set the cooler down, however, he frowned at a framework at one side of the picnic table. "Damn moose hunters been messing up my campsite again..."

"Moose hunters?" I echoed.

"Yeah. They hunt in the winter and mess up all the work I did maintaining the campsite over the summer so they can build crap like this to hang up the moose carcasses. I'll fix it in a minute. Let's get unpacked first." Hank set his side of the cooler down and began trudging back down the hill. "You coming? Three more coolers to go!"

I scowled and followed him back to the boats.

Jocelyn, as it turned out, had removed her lifejacket. I didn't know whether to thank or curse God that she'd sweated underneath it, plastering her light blue shirt against her chest.

"Mind the rope!" Hank barked, but it was too late. I tripped over the tie out and nearly landed flat on my face.

Hank sighed and clapped me on the shoulder as I got myself upright. "Son, I know the view's spectacular, but you need to pay attention and be careful around here. It's at least three hours to the nearest hospital."

The view? He wasn't—

No. Hank was pointing at an eagle's nest just past Jocelyn's shoulder. There was a bald eagle sitting in it and one perched further up the tree.

"Wow," I whispered.

"Majestic creatures," Hank agreed. "But they'll be there all week. We want to get camp set up so we can have a little something to eat and then go fishing."

I nodded and proceeded to help Hank with the last three coolers.

Before long, Hank and I had a large tarp up over the campsite, held up by strategically placed dead trees that Hank had hammered into the ground at some point like towering fence posts. There was also an A-line tarp over our gear.

While Hank encouraged the "womenfolk" to start putting up their tents, Hank and I erected the cook tent.

I could hear Mom giggling in the background, which told me she was being absolutely useless in getting the tent she would be sharing with Hank together. Once Hank and I finished with the cook tent, I saw it was just as I thought.

Mom was sitting between whippy tent poles, trying to bend them into place, but she'd fed them wrong in the first place, so nothing was happening. Hank just smiled indulgently and went to help her.

I went to find my own tent to put up a few feet away from theirs, only to see Jacey's was already standing across from mine, and she was kneeling on the ground, assembling mine, now.

"Thanks, Jocelyn," I said quietly, coming up behind her.

She jumped, then blushed. "Well, you know, you were getting all that other stuff done with Dad."

I peeked through the screen of Jocelyn's tent. "You've even got your cot up and your sleeping bag ready."

Jocelyn nodded. "I even unpacked a little. But don't unpack too much. I mean, we put tarps down inside the tents, but the floor can still get a little wet from ground water."

"Good to know," I said. I scrubbed my hand over the back of my neck. "Listen, Jocelyn, about what happened back at the landing..."

"What happened back at the landing?" Mom asked helpfully, popping her head over the brush between my tent and hers.

Shit.

"We had an argument," Jocelyn replied quickly. "When I went to bring him his bag."

Mom frowned. "Caleb. Jacey was doing something nice for you, and you got into an argument?"

"Are you trying to ruin this trip?" Hank pitched in, his head also coming into view.

I ground my teeth. I was pretty sure my dentist was going to need a microscope to find any enamel by the time we got home. "No. I didn't realize the bags were switched, so I was yelling at her for—"

"—almost catching him naked," Jocelyn finished quickly. "Luckily, he hadn't started changing yet."

"Oh. Well, you still shouldn't have yelled," Mom admonished me.

I looked at Jocelyn. "You're right. I shouldn't have yelled."

Jocelyn ducked her head and cleared her throat. "Anyway, do you still need help with your tent?"

Oh, I needed help with a tent alright, but not the one we were assembling. "Nah, I'm good. Thanks, Jocelyn."

"You're welcome." Jocelyn ducked into her tent and zipped the second flap closed, this one opaque so I couldn't see in.

"I wish you two would just get along," Mom sighed.

"You're going to have to," Hank said. "You're sharing a boat for ten days."

I knew it. That motherfucker.

CHAPTER 5: ONE BIG HAPPY

-Jacey-

My father started a fire, and soon we were roasting weenies on sticks. Jeanie and my father took one of the makeshift stump-and-board benches near the fire, so Caleb and I were forced side-by-side on the other.

Caleb was roasting his own weenie, and so was I, but my father had stuck two weenies on one stick and had his arms around Jeanie, teaching her to roast as though he were teaching her to golf. Jeanie giggled the whole time.

"Enjoying your birthday trip so far?" Caleb asked in a low tone as he slowly turned his weenie over the fire. They'd come cold, nearly frozen, from the cook tent cooler, so waiting for them to sizzle and split was a bit of a chore.

I set my jaw and didn't answer him. I didn't have to. Caleb knew that this was my worst birthday since I'd turned fifteen and foolishly confessed I had a crush on him.

Caleb gently bumped my shoulder with his. "I am sorry about before, Jocelyn."

"Hmph," I answered noncommittally.

He leaned closer to my ear. "And I'm sorry about your fifteenth birthday."

I was so startled, I dropped my stick, hotdog and all, in the fire.

My father groaned. "Jacey!"

"Oh dear. I'm sure I can make you a sandwich," Jeanie said brightly.

"That's wasteful. Does it look like we're anywhere near a Cub Foods?" my father complained.

Caleb stood before I could stop him. The expression on his face told me he might actually walk over and slug my father.

Instead, he deliberately dropped his stick in the middle of the fire.

"What do you want on your sandwich, Jocelyn?" Caleb asked me, turning his back and stalking towards the cook tent.

I stared, openmouthed. My father was so red, I wondered if Jeanie was going to try to smear HIM with sunscreen.

Caleb was looking back at me expectantly.

I had a choice here. I could back down and say I wasn't hungry and keep my father happy. Or I could show a little rebellion and go with Caleb.

It shocked the hell out of me when I rose to my feet and went after Caleb. Caleb smiled slightly at me and put an arm around my shoulders. It felt both protective and in solidarity.

"Hank, just let them have sandwiches. We packed plenty of food. You know that." Jeanie soothed my father over the crackling of the fire.

I could hear my father muttering words like "ungrateful" and "disobedient" and "bad influence," and it made me feel a bit better about the whole situation. I'd never admit it to Caleb, but I could admit it to myself: I was a bit pissed off at my father.

He'd made a huge deal about this happy family vacation for MY birthday but so far had just doted on Jeanie. He was also making Caleb's camping trip a living hell. As for me...

"Did you tell your dad you'd been hoping for your usual father/daughter trip this year for your birthday?" Caleb asked me softly, as though reading my thoughts. He pulled bread, Miracle Whip, ham, cheese, and a head of lettuce out of the cooler.

"Well... yeah," I admitted.

"He decided this was better?" Caleb said. He wiped off the folding table we'd recovered from my father's stash in the woods and began setting out a kind of sandwich station.

"I... think he wanted to show Jeanie this place," I replied.

Caleb paused. "A place just you and him shared? He didn't, I don't know, see there might be a problem with that?"

I drew a little circle in the dirt with my toe. I could feel Caleb's eyes on me, and my cheeks heated up. "He really wanted to have you and Jeanie celebrate with us. I don't know. It's not that big a deal."

"Bullshit." Caleb put together a sandwich while he shook his head and slapped it on a plate. He handed it to me.

"I don't eat—" I stopped, realizing he'd made my sandwich exactly the way I like it.

"You don't eat cheese," Caleb finished for me.

I nodded. "You remembered."

"Hard to forget. Don't worry, more for me," Caleb grinned, dropping two slices of cheese on his own sandwich.

I couldn't help it. I giggled.

Caleb smiled down at me with genuine warmth. Then something in his eyes changed, something that made me feel electrified inside and out.

"We should go sit down, Jocelyn," Caleb murmured. His eyes were on my lips once more.

I licked them.

Caleb leaned forward.

Just when I thought he might kiss me, Caleb leaned past me and grabbed the knife out of the Miracle Whip jar. He licked the white dressing off it slowly, his eyes locked on mine.

"We're playing a dangerous game," Caleb rumbled.

"What... what game?" I whispered. I could smell campfire on him, and that heady, dark scent that was uniquely Caleb.

Caleb's smile was slow and made my heart pound and my panties wet.

"You know what game." He took his sandwich out on a paper plate back to the fire.

I had to steady myself against the table for a moment before going back to sit next to him on the bench.

"All I can say is the fishing had better be good tomorrow," my father grunted, eyeing us and our sandwiches. "Because that's what we're eating."

"I'm sure the fishing will be great, Hank," Jeanie said, leaning against his arm. They were happily munching on their hotdogs.

"Sandwiches aren't bad, either." Caleb was needling my father.

"We won't be having sandwiches tomorrow," my father seethed.

Caleb opened his mouth to say some smartass remark, I was sure, but I bumped my knee against his.

"We'll see," my stepbrother amended.

When we finished our sandwiches, we threw our plates in the fire. My father stood and took Jeanie's hand, tugging her toward their tent.

"I thought we were going fishing?" I said.

Jeanie blushed and looked up at my father.

My father smiled down at her and then shrugged at me. "You and Caleb are welcome to go out in the canoe. There should be some good sunset fishing."

"Oh, okay," I replied, a bit disappointed. "I guess we'll just go out bright and early tomorrow morning, then."

"Well, you got the bright and early part right," my father said. "But you're going to be fishing with Caleb."

"Tomorrow?" I asked, surprised.

"All week," my father responded. "Somebody's got to show him the ropes."

"Even on my birthday?" I asked.

My father sighed. "Jacey, I wish you and your brother would just get along—"

"For Chrissake, she's not my sister," Caleb cut in, "and if you want time to fuck my mom, you should just say so. I'll take Jocelyn out in the boat. You two have fun tonight. But get your fucking head out of your fucking ass, you asshole. Jocelyn wanted to come here with you, to spend time with YOU for her birthday. And you can't be fucking bothered to take her out once?"

I stared at Caleb. So did my father.

Jeanie burst into tears. "Oh Jacey, I'm so sorry. I've ruined your birthday, haven't I?"

My father's expression turned positively thunderous. "How dare you speak to me that way? To your mother?!"

"Oh come on, you've been riding the bullshit wave all the way here, and I'm tired of it. You're deliberately pissing me off for your own twisted sense of fun because you think I'm not going to call you on your bullshit. You've been treating Jocelyn like crap. Does that make you feel like a big man in front of my mother, Hank?" Caleb yelled.

I thought they might actually come to blows. Jeanie was sobbing, tugging on my father's arm to stop him from stomping over to Caleb. I put my hands on Caleb's chest and pushed him back with all the strength I had when he took a step toward my father.

"Let's go fishing," I pleaded with Caleb. "Please, Caleb. Let's just go fishing."

"You'll be using Jacey's tackle because you won't be using a damn thing I bought you!" my father shouted after us as I slowly managed to get Caleb to walk backward.

"It's okay," I murmured. "I have two poles and plenty of tackle. Let's just go."

Caleb curled his lip at my father, but he let me take him by the wrist down to the canoe. True to his word, Caleb pulled his own tackle box out of the canoe and dropped it on the shore with a thud. His poles followed.

I winced. "Be nice to the equipment."

Caleb snorted but was nicer to the boat cushion and his lifejacket.

"We can't go without your lifejacket," I said sternly.

"Why not? Your dad bought it for me. And he said I wasn't going to be using any of his equipment," Caleb shot back.

I folded my arms over my chest. "My father didn't mean you shouldn't wear your lifejacket. Lifejackets are mandatory. I'm not going anywhere with you unless you put it on."

"Why, somebody die?" Caleb asked.

"Two men. Last year. And that's just who I know about. Right here, on this lake, swimming from this campsite..." I pointed back the way we'd come. "... to that shoreline." I indicated the shoreline across from us.

Caleb blinked, then obligingly clipped his lifejacket in place. "Shit. Your dad's not kidding about safety."

"We never kid about safety," I confirmed. I went to the rope and untied us, pushing the metal canoe out into the water as soon as Caleb was situated in the back.

Caleb started the motor in one pull this time and navigated us just far enough away from camp that we couldn't be seen. Then he turned to me. "How about you drive? I'll bet you know all the good fishing spots."

"I do. Most of them, anyway. I mean, there's TONS my dad knows about that we only go to once in a while that I couldn't tell you where they are, but the main honey holes, yeah, I know where they are," I said.

"Honey... holes?" Caleb repeated, his lips twitching.

Oh God. I knew I must be lobster red. "Well, that's what my dad calls them. See, walleye hang out in holes or drop-offs a lot of the time in twenty to twenty-five feet of water... so when you find just the right spot where you can pull fish almost all the time, it's called a honey hole."

"I'm gonna remember that one," Caleb chuckled. "Anyway, let's switch spots."

"Okay, but we've got to be careful," I said. "The canoe's a lot more tippy than the boat."

"Noted," Caleb replied as he leaned over and did a kind of crawl walk with his hands on the sides of the metal canoe, coming toward me.

He sat right in front of me at the bottom of the canoe so I could move out of my seat and maneuver around him. I crouched down and was just getting to my feet when we bumped a rock.

Caleb toppled backward, and I landed right on top of him, pelvis to pelvis, lifejacket to life jacket. If it hadn't been for those lifejackets, we'd have probably bumped noses, too. As it was, our faces were inches apart.

I licked my lips nervously, again.

"Really wish you wouldn't have done that," Caleb whispered as he captured my lips with his.

CHAPTER 6: BUMPING INTO OTHER

-Caleb-

Jocelyn's lips were just as soft and plump and perfect as I'd expected. The lifejackets were awkward as fuck, but I still managed to put a hand at the nape of her neck and keep her lips pressed to mine.

I felt it when the shock left her body and she melted into me. I flicked my tongue over her lips, asking for entry.

Jocelyn parted her lips with a little gasp, and I took the invitation and slid my tongue into her mouth.

Fuck, she tasted good. Like honey.

I got rock hard as I imagined what she tasted like other places as well.

My tongue massaged against hers, encouraging her. When she very tentatively tangled her tongue with mine, I knew beyond a shadow of a doubt that she didn't have a lot of experience with boys.

She was probably a virgin.

The thought had me groaning and pulling my lips away. While my dick twitched eagerly at the idea of being her first lover, my brain finally caught up and convinced me this was wrong.

"Caleb?" Jocelyn breathed, her chest rising and falling in rapid little pants.

I ran my thumb over her cheek and smiled sadly. "Jocelyn, I'm not going to touch you anymore."

Jocelyn's brow furrowed. "Why not?"

I thought maybe I might have scared her with my intensity, but no, not my Jocelyn. If she only knew what those deep green eyes invited.

I bumped my forehead to hers. "I don't think I'll be able to stop."

Jocelyn's eyes widened. "Oh."

"Yeah. Oh," I responded.

She contemplated that for a while, then licked her swollen lips.

My cock strained at the innocent motion.

"Is it okay if you didn't stop?" Jocelyn asked cautiously. "I mean... I don't mind."

I sighed and squeezed my eyes shut, telling my body to calm down. It didn't work. "Jocelyn, I will not have your first time happen in the bottom of a canoe."

Jocelyn stared at me. Then her cheeks flushed. "H-How did you know that?"

"That you're a virgin? Or that we're in a canoe?" I tried teasing.

It didn't calm my hard-on any, and it just made Jocelyn blush more. "The... virgin thing."

I ran my fingers over her braid. "I just know."

"Am I a bad kisser?" Jocelyn asked.

A bad kisser? I let out a bark of laughter. "Jocelyn, I'm sitting here with an erection that can probably be seen from space. Trust me. You kiss JUST fine."

"Oh." Jocelyn looked down, or at least attempted to, but our lifejackets were in the way.

"Mhm," I said. "So, if you wouldn't mind getting off me, I have to start thinking of grannies and cold showers."

Jocelyn laughed nervously and crawled the rest of the way over me to get to the back of the canoe. Her whole body skimmed right over my face.

I wasn't complaining, but it also wasn't helping the situation downstairs. I hooked my thumbs in the loops on my jeans to keep myself from reaching up to grab that beautiful, round ass of hers.

Once Jocelyn was settled, I moved to where she had been sitting. She navigated the canoe effortlessly to what I assumed was our first "honey hole."

I almost brought it up to see the tantalizing blush spread across her face again, but Jocelyn shoved a pole into my hands and opened her tackle box. She quickly chose tackle for me and baited my line, handling a dried minnow without flinching.

"I like watching you... do that," I murmured, grinning when she did, indeed, blush again. "But I really have been fishing before, and I can bait my own line."

"You haven't fished here. You wouldn't know what tackle to use," Jocelyn replied with a shrug. "We've also got worms and leeches."

"Good thing you're not squeamish," I teased.

Jocelyn laughed. "Never. I've been fishing too long for that. But I still wear a fish glove. Dad handles all his catches bare-handed."

"That's very manly of him," I deadpanned.

Jocelyn poked a finger in my direction. "Don't you go bashing my father. He's a good man."

I had my reservations, but I relented. "All right. No more dad-bashing."

"Good." Jocelyn dropped her line in the water and indicated for me to do the same. "I'm going to back-troll us around the honey—er—where they're usually sitting slowly. You're going to want to jig your line."

"It's all coming back to me," I assured her. I jigged the line slowly while Jocelyn got us moving backward, maneuvering the motor with one hand and her pole with the other. Her jigging was smooth and graceful. I felt clumsy by comparison.

"When's the last time you fished?" Jocelyn asked as we waited for a nibble.

"Hmm," I said, staring out at the beautiful shoreline. I remembered exactly when, but it wasn't something I liked to recall. "I guess when I was about twelve. My dad took me."

"Oh." Jocelyn was doing the math, and I knew she'd come to the right conclusion. "Right before he got cancer. I'm sorry."

I squared my shoulders. "No harm done."

"I still didn't mean to—"

There was a hard jerk on my line and my pole bent in an arc. "Looks like I got one!"

"Don't forget to set the hook!" Jocelyn said, reeling in her own line while I played my fish. She set her pole down and grabbed the net.

I glanced down, then looked again. "The net's purple."

"Oh. Yeah... it's my favorite color," Jocelyn mumbled.

I grinned. "Purple. I'll remember that." I hauled the fish up close to the boat, looked down, and laughed. "Don't bother with the net."

"Why not? It looked like it hit your line pretty hard," Jocelyn said.

I easily lifted a walleye not even a foot long and skinny into the air. "It's a monster."

Jocelyn bit her lip, but finally couldn't hold back a spurt of giggles. "You've got that right. I think his mouth is bigger than his whole body."

"I think you're right." I started trying to get the hook out of the little walleye's jaw.

"Caleb, no! Don't hold him like that, he has a—!"

It was too late. Even as Jocelyn tried to warn me, her explanation became pointedly clear. Literally.

The angry little walleye deployed his spiky, sharp back fan, and I sliced my palm open.

"Fuck!" I shouted, dropping the walleye to the bottom of the canoe.

Jocelyn quickly donned her fish glove and gripped the walleye before he could cause trouble. She dumped him overboard, then tossed her fish glove back into her tackle box and scooted carefully to the next seat forward in the canoe. "Is it bad?" she asked while I cradled my hand.

"Fuck me, that hurt. It's probably not as bad as it looks, though," I grumbled, feeling like an idiot.

Jocelyn took my hand in hers and wiped my blood away with her blue shirt. "It's not too deep? You're not squirting blood or anything, so it didn't hit an artery. Dad will know if it needs stitches."

"Great. I get to show your father I can't even catch a fish properly. Joy," I sighed.

"He's sliced his hand open, too. It happens. If I didn't have my fish glove, I'm sure I'd get cut open all the time," Jocelyn reassured me.

I still had a feeling I'd be getting my fair share of crap over this. But, Jocelyn was right. Better to be safe and go see the bastard than potentially get gangrene or something.

"Do you think they're done playing 'hide-the-salami'?" I asked sarcastically.

Jocelyn wrinkled her nose. "Ew. Gross."

"I'd rather not walk in on them, how about you?" I said.

"No..." Jocelyn replied, going a bit green. "But we have to have your hand looked at. They'll be able to hear the motor approaching."

"I hope," I muttered.

Jocelyn started going back to the motor, then stopped. "Take off your shirt."

"Excuse me?" I responded while my baser instincts began to perk up.

"Your shirt. Take it off," Jocelyn repeated.

I raised an eyebrow at her. "Does blood turn you on or something?"

Jocelyn rolled her eyes. "No. But we've got to put something around your hand to stop the bleeding, and my dad might get a bit testy if I take MY shirt off."

"I wouldn't mind..."

"Look. Whatever this is going on, whatever 'game' you think we're playing, it needs to go on hold for a minute because you're injured," Jocelyn said sternly.

I chuckled and unclipped my lifejacket, peeling off my shirt. The air was cool against my skin. But I could feel Jocelyn's hot gaze on my body. Even though she was trying to be businesslike now, I knew, and she knew, and I knew that she knew that I knew she was watching. There was a sharp intake of breath, then Jocelyn blushed and turned her head aside.

"Put your lifejacket back on," Jocelyn instructed hoarsely.

I leaned closer to her. "Eh? Can't hear you."

Jocelyn's blush deepened. "Caleb, we're not going anywhere until you have your lifejacket on."

"Okay, okay." I held up my hands in surrender and clipped the restrictive, camo-colored lifejacket back on. Jocelyn's was a neon purple, I observed. I'd been so busy trying to see through it that I hadn't clocked the color.

In fact, her tackle box and one of her fishing rods were also purple.

I chuckled as I wrapped my shirt around my bleeding hand. "Wow, you do have a purple fetish."

"Yes... well... everyone has a favorite color," Jocelyn said, putting the motor back in motion once I was settled.

We practically flew over the pristine, slate blue water back to camp. Once we arrived, Jocelyn let the boat glide to the shore. I jumped out and pulled it further onto shore with my good hand.

"I'll get the rope," Jocelyn told me, pointing up the incline toward camp. "You go tell my father you could use some help."

"I think I'd rather get gangrene," I grumbled, but trudged up to the campsite nonetheless.

Hank and Mom were sitting by the fire again, looking pleasantly disheveled. When Hank saw me, however, his expression darkened. "You weren't out there long."

I bit the inside of my cheek against a retort and held out my hand. "I had a misunderstanding with a walleye. He won."

Mom turned pale and jumped to her feet, running over to me. "Oh my God, Hank, he's bleeding!"

"Grabbed it wrong, didn't you," Hank said, unperturbed. He rose slowly and sauntered over to me. "Well, show me."

I unwound my shirt from my hand.

Hank took my hand in his and whistled. "Got you good. I'll get the first aid kit. Jeanie, nothing to worry about, darling. He just needs a bandage and some bacitracin."

Jocelyn came walking up the hill, then. "What's the verdict?" she asked.

"Verdict is your brother's an idiot," Hank snorted.

Gee, and just when I was beginning to think he might be a stand-up guy about all this. "Jocelyn told me you've been cut by a walleye, too."

"Sure have," Hank said. "But I know a cut like that only happens when you try grabbing one around the middle, and you'd only do that to a tiny little bastard. So you got beat by a minnow."

I couldn't stand his gloating. I snatched the supplies from him and plonked myself down on the picnic table bench. "I can take care of it myself, thanks."

Hank shrugged. "Suit yourself. Your mother and I are turning in for the night. Oh, I snore."

"Fantastic." As the evening sun was rapidly falling into night, I lit one of the kerosene lamps and brought it over next to me. The bacitracin step went fine, but as for wrapping the bandage...

Mom and Hank's tent zipped open, then back closed again. I figured I was on my own until Jocelyn cleared her throat.

"Want some help?" she asked.

I looked down at the mess I was making. "Probably a good idea."

Jocelyn straddled the bench next to me and took my hand, carefully wrapping it. "Dad really does think he's just being funny."

"He isn't," I growled.

"I know. But he thinks he is." Jocelyn laid my hand on my thigh.

I took her hand before she could pull it away. "Thanks." I played my thumb over the lines on her palm, rubbing slow circles.

Jocelyn looked behind us and dropped her voice. "Caleb, they're right behind us."

"Unless they have X-ray vision, that's not a problem," I replied, still rubbing circles.

"Caleb..."

I sighed and brought Jocelyn's palm to my mouth for a kiss before releasing her. "I know this is all getting really confusing, really quickly. We'll talk more about it tomorrow, okay?"

Jocelyn nodded then quickly clomp-clomped in her wader boots to her tent.

I leaned back and looked at the sky, wondering how long it would be before the stars came out. I supposed if I waited long enough, I might be able to figure out what to do about Jocelyn.

CHAPTER 7: MIDNIGHT HEAT

-Jacey-

Caleb had kissed me.

The thought rolled around and around in my mind.

Caleb had kissed me.

Caleb had kissed me!

Sure, the events that followed after had momentarily washed the desire and confusion from me, but now that I was alone on my cot, there was nothing to do but think about his firm, inquisitive lips on mine.

He'd also put his tongue in my mouth, which had caused a burst of sensations I hadn't even known I was capable of.

The heat ratcheted up when I remembered I'd also given him a hard-on. Me!

Even though the temperature had fallen overnight, and I should be happily cocooned in my sleeping bag, I couldn't stand the heat. I was laying on top of my sleeping bag now, remembering the kiss that had started this fire in me.

I sawed my legs together, the heat going exactly where I didn't want it. It was delicious, but our parents were ten feet from my tent.

There was a shorter distance between my tent and Caleb's. I couldn't give myself sweet relief.

Frustrated, I sat up on the cot and felt around for my shoes. After pulling them on, I felt for my flashlight and then headed for the flap of my tent. I quietly opened the flap and screen, only to realize the flashlight wouldn't be necessary. It was a full moon, and the stars were bright enough to light the way.

Our campsite was different than others in the Canadian wilds in that my father had built and hidden a wooden port-a-potty closer to the top of the hill in the trees. I trudged up the path, watching for roots and stones.

I didn't realize someone else was there until I smacked right into a wall of naked chest. I dropped my flashlight, and it rolled somewhere into the night.

"Jocelyn?" a familiar voice whispered, reaching out and grabbing my upper arms to steady me.

"Caleb?" I looked up and, sure enough, I was facing my stepbrother. Worse, I had my hands on his bare chest.

It was too dark to see the color of his eyes, but there was a glimmer in them in the starlight. "Going to the john?" he asked.

I nodded dumbly.

"Well, it's free. But I accidentally knocked the toilet paper down, so I was getting another roll. You might want to wait a minute..." Caleb said. But then, he didn't move, or take his hands off me.

His thumb traced the spaghetti strap of my cotton camisole. I blushed, realizing I was standing in front of him in an old Care Bears camisole and shorts set. A more sophisticated woman would have brought some kind of lacy lingerie, but not me.

I could only pray he couldn't see the pattern in the dark.

"Wish Bear?" Caleb chuckled softly.

My cheeks heated up. "Yes, well, seems appropriate for pajamas."

Caleb flicked his eyes down the short path to where our tents were set up. "You know, if our parents come wandering out, this might look a little compromising."

"Huh?" I asked.

Caleb looked down, and I realized my hands were still pressed against his bare chest.

"Oh crap." I carefully lifted my hands away.

Caleb caught my wrist, tugging me back up the path, past the outhouse and further into the woods.

"Where are we going?" I asked, stumbling after him.

"Somewhere where prying ears can't see and prying ears can't hear," Caleb said. "Though, Hank's snoring could cover an air raid."

When he deemed we'd gone far enough, Caleb pushed me back against the pale, papery bark of a birch tree. "We have to decide what we're doing here."

"Doing?" I squeaked, feeling Caleb's hot eyes on me, even in the dark.

Caleb leaned an arm against the birch tree, looming right into my space. We were breathing the same breaths. "You know what I'm talking about, Jocelyn."

My heart thudded erratically in my chest. "I... don't understand what's going on, honestly. I thought you hated me."

"No such luck," Caleb said with a sardonic smile, his teeth white against the dark. "I've wanted you since you first told me you love me. But... I was older than you and I needed to do the adult thing and stay away."

"You're still older than me," I pointed out softly.

Caleb smoothed a strand of hair behind my ear, following the motion through to cup my cheek and run his thumb over my lower lip. "You'll be eighteen the day after tomorrow."

"Age of consent in Minnesota is sixteen," I told him.

Caleb had to hush his hearty laugh. "Looked this up before, have you?"

"Maybe," I mumbled, dropping my eyes.

"Good to know, but I still won't have sex with you for at least two days," Caleb said. He played his fingers down over my throat softly, then lower until they were drawing a heated line between my breasts.

I thought I might spontaneously combust.

"Do you want that?" Caleb asked.

"Want...?" I echoed hazily.

Caleb nuzzled my ear. "Do you want me to be your first?"

If the tree wasn't there, I may have swooned. As it was, I had to squeeze some sense out of my brain if I was really going to have this conversation with Caleb.

"I... I wouldn't... I wouldn't want you to be my first, unless there was a possibility that you would also be my last," I managed to gasp.

Caleb arched an eyebrow at me. "You're a romantic."

"Yes," I said defensively.

"Hmm. That surprises me." Caleb regarded me for a long moment. "What happened with your mom..."

I stiffened. I couldn't believe he was bringing up my mother! "What does she have to do with anything?"

Caleb's expression lost its seductiveness, and he took a small step backward. "Jocelyn, I'm sorry if I hit a nerve. But I figured since she left you—"

"Don't." I held up a hand. "Don't bother. I don't want to hear the rest of that explanation." I shoved past him and headed back down the hill.

"Jocelyn!" Caleb called softly after me.

I stormed to my tent, yanking the zipper up so hard I almost took the zip right off the teeth. I zipped the flap and the screen shut.

To his credit, Caleb was not stupid enough to try to pursue me all the way to my tent. I heard him trudge to his own and go inside, zipping it closed.

I couldn't believe I'd ever found him attractive. Okay, I still found him attractive, but I was going to work on that.

Just because my mother left us when I was five, that meant I wasn't supposed to be a romantic? That I'd want to just sleep around? That I'd want to be Caleb's fuck toy?

Was I somehow worth less because my mother had left, but his father had died?

I couldn't stop fuming. Tears of anger and frustration stung my eyes into the wee hours of the morning when my father came over and shook my tent.

"Rise and shine, cupcake! It's time to help me make breakfast," he said.

I dragged myself out of my sleeping bag and pulled on real clothes—a sweatshirt and jeans. Then I walked out in a pair of tennis shoes to help my father.

"So," my father grinned, while mixing pancake batter, "you were up late last night."

"Huh?" I replied. "What do you mean?" How did he know? WHAT did he know?!

Not that there was really anything to know. Not anymore.

My father reached into his pocket and pulled out my flashlight. "Must have lost this when you were walking up to the john."

"Oh. Yeah." I took the flashlight and slipped it into my pocket while I toasted bread over the camp stove.

"Is it your... you know... time of the month?" my father asked, just as Caleb walked toward the cook tent.

Oh God. "No." I was sure I was scarlet from head to toe.

"It's just all the toilet paper I had up there last night is gone," my father explained.

"I bumped it by accident, and it fell in the toilet," Caleb said, saving me from further embarrassment.

Perhaps I wouldn't resolve to hate him for ALL eternity.

My father scowled at Caleb. "That's very wasteful, son."

Caleb scowled right back. "I'm not your son."

As I was trying to figure out how to avert a fight between them, the toast I'd stopped paying attention to started smoking.

"Jacey!" my father cried, taking a tongs and yanking the wire toasting ring off the burner. "Goddammit, TWO meals in a row?!"

"Sorry, Dad. I wasn't paying attention," I said with a wince.

"Will you stop fucking yelling at her all the time? Jesus, it's supposed to be her fucking birthday celebration or some shit," Caleb snapped.

"Caleb, why are you shouting?" Jeanie asked, sticking her head out of the tent she shared with my father.

Caleb snorted. "Of course. Mom gets to sleep but make sure

Jocelyn is helping in the kitchen."

"I like helping," I defended my father's decision.

Jeanie's eyes welled up again. "Please don't fight. We're supposed to be having a nice family vacation."

"Then tell your husband to stop being a prick!" Caleb yelled so loud even the seagulls were scared off.

"Guess somebody doesn't want breakfast," my father seethed.

"Guess somebody's on a hell of a power trip," Caleb shot back.

Jeanie wrung her hands and looked at me as though there was something I could do.

Honestly, I was just tired. Tired of all of it. I walked out of the cook tent and down to the shoreline. "I'll be back later!" I called up to camp as I untied the canoe and stepped into it.

"Wait, Jacey. We haven't finished breakfast!" my father called back down.

"I can help with breakfast," Jeanie said, her voice soft on the wind.

"Jeanie, darling, you're a guest. Why don't you get a little more sleep?" My father's reply made my blood boil.

Apparently, it did Caleb's as well, because before I could push off, my stepbrother came tromping down the path. "I'm coming with you. Don't argue. We don't have to talk. But I'm getting the fuck out of here."

I took one look at Caleb's face and decided I wouldn't argue. "Can you shove us off?" I asked.

"Can I run the motor, actually?" Caleb replied.

"Seriously? I'm the one trying to escape, and you want to—"

Caleb raked a hand over his hair and gave me a pleading look. "Please?"

I sighed and got out of the canoe so Caleb could crawl in the back. Then I shoved us off.

Caleb started the motor just as my father came thumping down to the beach.

"You two—!" he said, stabbing a finger at us.

With a sneer, Caleb opened the motor up full bore, and we went pelting across the lake.

CHAPTER 8: ACCIDENTS HAPPEN

-Caleb-

"Caleb, we need to slow down," Jocelyn said after about a minute.

We were wearing life jackets, because Jocelyn insisted again. I could still see camp from where we were, so I shook my head. "No can do. If I squint one eye, I could probably see your father flipping me the bird."

"He... okay, he might actually do that... but there are rocks out in the middle of the lake here in some places, too, you know!" Jocelyn yelled over the sound of the motor.

"We'll be fine," I grunted, maneuvering the canoe around a corner.

Jocelyn gripped the sides of the canoe, her eyes wide with fear. "Caleb—"

"Weren't we going to be quiet?" I snapped.

Jocelyn lapsed into silence, but her knuckles were white on the sides of the canoe.

I sighed and slowed down. "I just want to get away, okay? Just for a while."

"It'll be kinda permanent if we both die out here," Jocelyn pointed out.

I gave a bitter laugh. "True. Shit, between your dad and I, we're really ruining your birthday. I'm sorry, Jocelyn."

Jocelyn shrugged. "It's fine. It is what it is."

"It's not fine." I held up my hands when she frowned at me. "But we'll agree to disagree."

"Sounds good." Jocelyn lapsed back into silence.

I kept us going through the water. Clouds began rolling in from the northeast..

"We've got rain gear in here, right?" I asked Jocelyn once the clouds started getting darker.

Jocelyn looked at the sky, then bit her lip. "Sorry, I wasn't paying attention to where we were going. Do you know where camp is from here? I've never been to this part of the lake before."

Indeed, I had also lost track of time. We'd been traveling for at least two hours. I swallowed hard and said, "Jocelyn, I have no idea where camp is from here."

"Oh crap," Jocelyn murmured. "Oh crap, crap, crap."

"Should I pull off on an island somewhere?" I asked.

We both looked at the rocky, impassable shorelines around us. There wasn't an inch of sand to be seen.

The wind picked up, whipping wisps of Jocelyn's hair around her face as she gripped the sides of the canoe, looking for the same thing I was looking for—a friendly shore.

"We can just go back through the rain, right?" I suggested.

"Back where, Caleb? Neither of us knows where we are," Jocelyn replied miserably.

I felt one drop of rain on my nose then looked up just in time to be pelted by a gray storm. I'd walked under waterfalls with less force.

The canoe rocked as the wind blew harder, sending rolling waves across the big lake that threatened to capsize us.

The water was no longer a friendly slate blue, but a deathly gray-black.

"What do I do, Jocelyn?" I asked. "What do I do?"

"Turn the nose into the waves," Jocelyn said, obviously trying to keep calm. "Then see if you can navigate us between some islands. The water will be calmer there."

"Okay!" I responded above the storm.

We were both soaked, neither of us going for our rain gear. The canoe was pitching too much for us to have any success at putting it on anyway.

I pointed the nose at the crests of the waves, and the canoe slammed down several times between crests. It was bone-jarring and frightening as hell.

"Jocelyn, I can't see a damn thing in this rain!" I yelled.

"Rock! Rock, go right! Rock, rock, rock!" Jocelyn shouted back.

I tried, but the canoe smashed full sideways into a large, underwater rock whose tip could only be seen between waves. The canoe pitched onto its side, tossing Jocelyn, me, and all our gear out into the open water.

The lifejacket Jocelyn had insisted I always wear probably saved me from certain death. As it was, by the time I managed to get and keep my head above the waves, the canoe had been spun too far off for me to catch it.

My wader boots began to fill with water, weighing me down, so, with little choice, I kicked them off.

"Jocelyn!" I called into the storm. "Jocelyn?!"

A flash of neon purple a few yards away caught my attention. Distracted, I coughed and sputtered as a wave pounded over my head. When I bobbed back up, I sought out the purple again, then began swimming that way as best I could.

It was a long slog fighting the waves. I had to swim more sideways than straight ahead. But eventually, I made it to Jocelyn.

"Jocelyn?" I asked, grabbing her lifejacket.

Her head lolled to the side, and there was a pretty good gash on her forehead.

"Jesus. Jesus FUCK!" I swore, gripping the back strap on her life jacket and pulling her with me as I set out for shore—any shore.

I turned my back to the waves and let them carry us. It didn't take long before I saw trees ahead.

"Thank fuck," I said just before my socked foot connected with a sharp rock. "SONOFABITCH!"

The waves still bashed us forward. Jocelyn was limp on her back, so with some maneuvering, I was able to keep her from sustaining more injuries. But I could feel rock digging into my shins and knees.

Once we were close enough to shore, I began hauling Jocelyn over the rocks to the shoreline past them. It was dangerous going with the slippery rocks, but there was little other choice.

I didn't know what damage I'd done to my feet, shins, knees, and hands, but I finally clawed us past the rocks onto the shore. Past the rock was ground covered in dried pine needles and dirt, undisturbed by man.

If I'd been thinking about it at the time, I would have considered it a bad sign. But I had Jocelyn to worry about.

"Jocelyn?" I asked, ripping open her lifejacket and putting my ear to her chest.

She wasn't breathing, but she had a heartbeat.

I cupped my hands together and began CPR, pressing down on her ribcage.

"Please..." I begged whatever God would listen. "Please... Jocelyn... come back to me."

After a few more pumps, Jocelyn coughed and threw up water.

I moved her onto her side so she didn't choke, rubbing her back while she coughed the water out.

She rested a moment afterward, then turned her head slightly. "Caleb?" she asked.

"Yeah, I'm here. I'm here, Jocelyn," I reassured her.

"Why do you call me Jocelyn?" she mumbled.

She didn't seem to be quite "with it" yet, but I humored her just the same. "Because it's your name."

"S'not what people call me," Jocelyn said, resting her head on the bed of pine needles.

"Would you rather I call you Jacey?" I asked, curious.

Joselyn nodded. "Makes us closer." She started to nod off.

I shook her. "Nope, sorry, Jacey. You have to stay awake until we can figure out if you have a concussion."

"But I'm tired," Jocelyn whined.

"I know. You still have to stay awake, though," I responded.

Jocelyn let out the cutest little grunt of displeasure.

"You hit your head pretty good," I explained.

"Hurts." Jocelyn looked at me, her eyelashes getting wet in the rain. "Any gear?"

"Couldn't even grab the canoe," I sighed. "Guess we're stranded."

"Ugh." Jocelyn squeezed her eyes shut but opened them again before I gave her another shake.

I took off my lifejacket, folded it up, and put it under her head.

"That's a bit cold and wet," Jocelyn complained.

I chuckled. "We're both cold and wet. We're a couple of drowned rats."

Jocelyn clumsily patted my hand. "Thanks."

"Yeah, no problem. Just stay awake for now." I wished I could do something about hers and my wet clothes, but with the rain still pouring down, there was nothing for it but to be miserable.

It was getting quite cold, and I began looking around for something we could use to make a fire. But everything was wet in the rain. I grimaced.

"You know, I'm allowed to be a romantic," Jocelyn said, drawing my attention once more.

I winced. "Yeah, Jacey, I'm sorry about that. I didn't mean to imply anything—"

"Yes, you did. But I want to let you know right now, I'm allowed to be a romantic, even though my mom left. Just like you're allowed to be an asshole even though your parents had a great marriage before your father died," Jocelyn muttered.

I really had stuck my foot in it, and I wasn't sure how to heal the divide. Usually, I'd have gone silent a while, but the combination of the cold and what I suspected was a concussion kept trying to lull Jocelyn to sleep. "I'm sorry you think I'm an asshole."

"I thought you were hot," Jocelyn said. "I still think you're hot. And you used to be nice to me. But then you became an asshole. And then I thought you were starting to be nice again, and then you thought I was just some... some... some..."

"I didn't think anything like that, whatever you think I thought you were," I argued. "I was just surprised. That's all."

Jocelyn frowned at me, her eyes a bit unfocused. "You wanted me to be easy. You expected it, even."

That assessment hit me like a punch in the gut. I had been treating Jocelyn as though I expected her to be easy, ever since she'd seen me naked in the woods and telegraphed her clear desire for me. I should have known better. Jocelyn deserved better.

"Look," I said. "I have had a hard-on for you since the second you confessed you liked me at your fifteenth birthday. Which, I know I didn't handle well. And I'm sorry. I'm sorry I keep ruining your birthdays. This one is going to be another one for the books."

"Stranded with my stepbrother?" Jocelyn laughed weakly.

"Exactly," I sighed. "We may be well and truly fucked, Jacey."

"In that case, can I go to sleep?" Jocelyn teased.

I frowned at her. "Oh, ha-ha. No."

"The temperature is going to drop, maybe to the forties, maybe lower tonight," Jocelyn said softly. "What if no one finds us by then?"

When she spoke, I could faintly see her breath. The temperature had dropped further because of the storm. It made me shiver. "Let's just survive the rain first, shall we?" I replied, hugging my arms around myself.

Jocelyn nodded. Her eyes got heavy again, and I tried to think of something we could talk about that would keep her awake.

"Hey," I said, squeezing her hand. "No sleeping, remember?"

"But I'm so tired," Jocelyn whimpered.

"I know, Jacey, but you've got to tough it out. Tell me... tell me... uh... what do you remember about your mother?" I tried, going off our earlier subject.

Jocelyn wrinkled her brow. "She... left when I was five."

"Yeah, I know. But you must remember some stuff," I pressed. I'd started to shiver uncontrollably in the rain, and worried Jocelyn would start doing the same soon.

"She..." Jocelyn concentrated. "She smelled like... lilacs. It must have been her perfume or body lotion or something. She and my dad fought a lot. I remember a lot of yelling."

"I'm sorry about that," I murmured. "Maybe I should have chosen a different topic. I mean, are there any good things you remember about her?"

Jocelyn looked sad. "I'm not sure she wanted to be a mom. But I think she tried her best."

"Shit. Okay, new subject..." I said, wracking my brain.

"How about your dad? What was he like?" Jocelyn asked.

I'd completely opened a can of worms between us. She didn't want to talk about her mother because it seemed the woman had been a bit of a disappointment. But then how could she not be when she'd abandoned her own kid? In my case, I wasn't too keen on talking about my father because... well... I missed him.

"He used to rent a cabin in Wisconsin every year so we could go fishing. Little fish. Nothing like what your dad says you pull out of here," I said slowly. "I remember, when I was little, he liked to toss me in the air or zoom me around like an airplane. He was a huge Vikings fan. He loved my mom like crazy, and me, too."

"You must miss him," Jocelyn whispered.

I swallowed thickly and nodded. "I do."

"Is that why you don't like my dad?" Jocelyn asked.

"I like how your dad treats my mom. That's enough, I guess," I said carefully.

Jacey shook her head then winced at whatever pain that caused her. "There's more. You don't like him. I know it."

I fought to find the right words that would explain the situation, yet not make Jocelyn angry and defensive about her father. "I don't like how he dicks around with me."

"That's just his sense of humor. He doesn't mean to be insensitive; he just is," Jocelyn explained. "He's kind of like a puppy who pees on the carpet without knowing they did anything wrong."

"You're very forgiving, Jacey." I sighed and drew my knees to my chest, trying to conserve warmth. "Especially when I see how he treats you."

"What do you mean?" Jacey asked.

I could feel my nostrils flare as anger curled deep in my belly. "Like this trip. He did what he wanted instead of what you wanted, even though it's YOUR birthday. Things like that. If you were mine, it would matter to me what you feel and what you think. A lot."

"If I were your kid? You're only four years older than me, Caleb," Jocelyn snorted.

I leaned close and pressed my hand against her wet cheek. "No. Not if you were my kid. If you were my lover."

CHAPTER 9: LOST IN THE WOODS

-JACEY-

It was freezing, so cold that Caleb's warm hand on my numb, wet cheek actually stung. That was not, however, the place where most of the warmth in my body was bubbling up from. My heart beat a ba-thump ba-thump when he touched me, and his words touched a broken place in my soul.

I blinked, pretending my tears were just the rain that kept pouring on us. Or at least I could have if the rain hadn't, inconveniently, chosen just that moment to stop.

Caleb rubbed the tears under my eyes with his thumb, not saying a word. Even though we were both shivering so hard our teeth were chattering, he was still trying to take care of me.

"Please tell me you're not being so nice to me just to get into my pants," I mumbled, wincing at the pounding in my head when I tilted it a bit to see his face better.

"No," Caleb replied, sounding wounded. "I would never do that, Jacey."

"Okay." I accepted his answer, not because I was too tired to argue, but because I was willing to give him the benefit of the doubt. He had pulled me out of the water, after all. He had to have. There wasn't anyone else around.

I carefully scanned my eyes down his wet T-shirt that was plastered to bluish skin, hoping he hadn't been injured as well. Then I saw his crossed legs and gasped.

"Oh my GOD, Caleb! You're bleeding!" I cried. I tried to sit upright, but the world swam, and I groaned.

Caleb pressed my shoulders to settle me back down. "Yeah, I'll deal with that in a minute. You just keep still for a bit."

"You have no shoes!" I added. "Where are your boots? God, how did you get over the rocks?! It must have hurt like hell!"

"It didn't tickle, but I'm really okay. Some scrapes and bruises. We can deal with it. But you probably have a concussion," Caleb said.

"Well, Dr. Killeen, what do you suggest we do?" I sighed, frustrated I couldn't get up and help him.

"I think we're going to have to stay right here for a bit. They always say when you're lost, you shouldn't change locations so rescuers can find you," Caleb replied.

I nodded. "I can't argue with that logic. I can't get up to go anywhere right now anyway."

"Exactly," Caleb said. He groaned as he stood, wobbling on his feet a moment before finding balance. "Don't get any ideas," Caleb managed to grin as he started stripping off his pants.

His boxers left nothing to the imagination, and I'd heard somewhere cold water was supposed to make it shrink, but Caleb still had a monster of a cock. Then he peeled his jeans lower and pulled off his socks, and I saw the cuts and bruises on his knees, shins, and feet.

"We should dry our clothes," I suggested. "Then you can use your shirt and mine to bind some of that up."

Sure enough, as the weather had a tendency to do on the lake, the clouds had rolled away, and the sun was peaking in the sky, heating the air once more.

Caleb looked around for some obliging, low-hanging tree branches and hung up his holey jeans. He stripped his shirt off next and hung that up as well.

I tried to wriggle out of my clothes myself, but my head protested so much that I gave up with a moan. Caleb walked over to me and knelt beside me in the dirt, despite his wounds, and pulled off my boots, one at a time. Water poured out of them, but at least I still had them. I had no idea what Caleb was going to do.

The throbbing in my head did not allow me to appreciate Caleb's strong hands unzipping my jeans and peeling them down my legs.

"Funshine Bear?" Caleb teased when he caught sight of my bikini briefs.

"Shut up," I mumbled, feeling my cheeks heat up.

"No complaints. I think it's cute." Caleb then peeled off my shirt.

I was happy that my bra, at least, was a nice, white one. Nothing too showy, not too much lace—I mean, I packed for fishing, not potential sex with my stepbrother—but not ratty or covered with Care Bears.

Unfortunately, my nipples were freezing in the wet shirt, so when Caleb removed it, they were standing at pert attention.

Caleb zeroed right in on them, pausing as he held my clothes in his arms.

I covered my face with my hand and groaned. "This day just keeps getting better."

"It is from my perspective," Caleb chuckled.

I took a tired swat at him.

Caleb laughed more and stood to hang my clothes to dry as well.

When he returned to my side, Caleb sat down cross-legged on the ground. I frowned at his dirty wounds.

"You should go down to the lake and rinse those off," I said. "I can't believe you knelt on that."

Caleb shrugged. "Didn't hurt any more than it already did. But okay, if you say so."

"I do say so," I insisted.

Caleb smoothed back the wisps of my hair with a smile then went down to the water while butterflies fluttered around my stomach. I watched his toned back as he sat down on a rock and cupped water over his shins and knees.

I was so absorbed, I almost didn't hear the whuffling sound to my right. I turned my head and just barely managed to bite back a scream.

The abortive noise I did make, however, brought Caleb's attention up. "Holy shit!" I heard him say.

A black bear was making its way toward us, lumbering slowly.

"Okay..." I whispered, my chest rising and falling rapidly. "Okay... so... we don't have anywhere to go—"

Caleb reached into the lake beneath him and pulled out a fist-sized stone. He lobbed it at the bear. "FUCK OFF!" he shouted.

I stopped breathing altogether as the rock hit the bear squarely between the eyes.

The bear let out an angry snort but went loping back the way it came.

"Why the hell did you do that?!" I demanded, turning back to Caleb.

"Basic survival. You've been going up here all these years and never learned what to do when a black bear approaches you? It wasn't like we could back away anywhere," Caleb said. "Still, I don't want to stick around here and wait for that guy to come back."

I sat up, feeling a bit woozy, but better than I had the last time I tried. "I think... I think maybe I can stand..."

Caleb shook his head. "Let's not chance it."

"Well, what else are we going to d—" Before I could finish my question, Caleb had swept me up in his arms.

"We'll come back for our clothes later. Let's just get away from the water so our bear friend can have a drink or a swim or whatever he wants to do," Caleb grunted.

I wrapped my arms around Caleb's neck. "You do know you're barefoot, right?"

"I don't think your boots are going to fit me, Jacey," Caleb grinned.

"No, I know, I just... after the rocks and everything..." I said.

Caleb planted a soft kiss on my lips that zinged through me and caused all kinds of confusion in my muddled mind. "I'll be careful."

True to his word, Caleb did not go running into the woods. He picked his way carefully with me in his arms, always watching the ground ahead of us before taking his next steps.

As our bodies dried off, I became more and more aware that I was skin-to-skin and nearly naked with Caleb. I blushed in consternation and buried my face against his neck so he couldn't see.

"You're pink," Caleb said anyway, and I groaned.

"Sunburn," I tried.

"Not so much, but you go with that if you want to." Caleb kept us moving slowly through the trees.

"Your mom thought it was," I muttered.

"My mom couldn't conceive of the idea that you and I might be attracted to each other," Caleb pointed out.

I bit my lip and raised my head, looking Caleb in his beautiful blue eyes. "Is it... gross?"

Caleb stopped walking. "Do you think it's gross?"

"No. I mean, I never have. We met when I was thirteen and you were seventeen. It's not like we're blood related or anything," I mumbled, my eyes flicking away momentarily. "It's just that your mom seems to think it would be gross, and I didn't know what you thought."

"Jacey, look at me." Caleb pulled my attention back to him. "In the many, many, MANY times I've fantasized about being with you, it's been anything but gross. Unconventional, maybe, but never gross."

My whole body heated up, and I knew I was a bit more than pink now. "You fantasize about me?"

"You don't fantasize about me?" Caleb countered.

I swallowed. "Maybe."

"Maybe, she says. Maybe," Caleb chuckled. "Well, just so you know, seeing you nearly naked like this is going to keep my spank bank full for a while."

"Um, gross." But I giggled just the same.

Caleb put his mouth right up against my ear. "Do you touch yourself at night when you think about me?"

I shivered. "W-Weren't we worried about a bear?"

"I'll take that as a 'yes,'" Caleb said smugly.

I groaned and buried my face in his neck again.

Caleb shifted my weight, then started moving again. "You know I... oh. Hey, Jacey, look, do you see what I see?"

I looked up and scanned the woods. Then my eyes fell on the small hunting cabin Caleb must have been referring to. "It's... a cabin!"

"Yes!" Caleb picked up his pace.

"Caleb! Be careful," I admonished him.

Caleb sighed and slowed down a bit. "Maybe there's somebody home?"

"Probably not. It's not moose hunting season yet," I explained.

"But we can try," Caleb said excitedly. "If nothing else, it's shelter!"

"True," I agreed.

Caleb set me down carefully on the ground as soon as we got to the door of the cabin and knocked. Then he knocked again.

As I expected, there was no answer.

Caleb tried the knob, and the door opened. He poked his head inside. "Sweet, there's water and canned food in here!"

My stomach took that opportunity to rumble.

"Good thing, huh?" Caleb winked at me.

I folded my hands over my empty stomach. "I could have gone a little while without food," I said defensively.

Caleb's smile fell right off his face. "Hey. You're beautiful. Don't even think about not eating."

I rolled my eyes. "Yes, Dad."

Caleb grabbed my arm. "I mean it, Jacey. You're not going to starve yourself on my watch."

I sighed. "Caleb, I know you're trying to help, but that's not how it works. I'm in treatment. I'm doing a lot better. But it's really hard to change my thoughts, and it's not something you can do for me."

With a sad smile, Caleb kissed my forehead. "I sure wish I could, though."

"I know. I appreciate that, I do. But it's something I have to do for myself," I said.

Caleb nodded and released my arm. "Okay. I get that. But I'm still going to try to shove..." He picked up a can and read the label. "...creamed corn down you."

I wrinkled my nose. "Ew."

"Yeah, I agree. THAT is gross," Caleb grinned.

We stepped fully into the one-room cabin, and Caleb closed the door behind us. "Hey, why don't you go lay down while I see what's to be had in the pantry. Hopefully it's not just creamed corn, but you know what they say about choosy beggars."

"True," I replied. I walked across the dusty floorboards to the bed, coughing as a plume of dust went up when I laid down.

"Okay, could use a little airing out," Caleb observed. Then he triumphantly pumped his arm in the air, holding a can. "Beef stew!"

"Excellent," I said. "Let's have some of that. I don't suppose there's a range and some gas in here?"

Caleb looked around. "It looks like there's a table where they should be sitting, but I guess since the hunter's not here, he took it home."

"Cold stew it is." I shrugged.

After hunting around a bit, Caleb found a can opener.

Soon, we were eating cold beef stew out of the can, sitting side by side on the small bed.

"I thought your dad said there wouldn't be cabins on the lake? Something about the Canadian government and public property and all that," Caleb said after we finished.

"There's two or three cabins you can see from the lake. Dad says they were grandfathered in when the Canadian government basically declared this area public land," I replied. "We were lucky to find this place."

"Yeah. Damn lucky," Caleb agreed. He took the can and stood. "I'm going to go rinse this out and set it closer to the lake so we don't attract bears. Then I'll be back with our clothes."

I frowned. "What about the bear?"

"By now, he's probably done what he needs to do. Don't worry, I'll be careful," Caleb said.

Impulsively, I gave him a strong hug. "Come back in one piece, okay?"

Caleb chuckled and kissed my nose. "I promise. Don't go to sleep."

"Okay," I promised as well.

CHAPTER 10: OUR LITTLE BUBBLE

-Jacey-

I waited while Caleb took our silverware and the empty can down to the lake, praying he didn't get lost on the way back. The sun was just starting to dip down from its peak outside the window, and I knew my father and Jeanie probably wouldn't even be worried about our absence until sunset.

The silence without Caleb was maddening. It made me even more nervous about whether or not he was okay out there. He was wandering around in boxers, for God's sake.

I didn't know what time it was, but after a while, I decided it was taking too long. I stood up from the bed and started towards the door.

It opened just as I was reaching for the knob, and there was Caleb with two spoons in his hand, and nothing else but his boxers.

"The wind took the clothes," Caleb said in frustration, crowding me back into the room.

"Crap." I wandered back over to the bed and plunked down on it. "No sign of anyone on the lake?"

"I didn't see anybody. I got some rocks and spelled out 'HELP' back where we were, but I don't think you can see it from the lake."

Caleb sat down next to me and put an arm around my waist. "I don't know how anyone's going to find us."

"Maybe a ranger will come by," I replied hopefully.

Caleb raked a hand over his hair. "Yeah, maybe."

I put a hand on his thigh. "Look. Don't be discouraged. If nothing else, we can survive in this cabin for a while. Maybe the hunter will come in early moose hunting season. That's only like three weeks away. Maybe four."

Caleb looked down at his bare thigh with my hand on it and put his warm hand over mine. "I suppose a ranger will be by here within four weeks, even if the moose hunter doesn't come."

"Exactly," I said, swallowing. Caleb's thigh was firm and muscular. "Do you work out or something?"

"What?" Caleb asked, looking down at me.

"You're just all... muscle-y," I responded lamely.

Caleb took his hand off mine to brush my cheek, framing the side of my face with his hand. "Do you like that, Jacey?"

"Y-Yes," I admitted, not sounding quite as bold as I wanted to.

Caleb ran his thumb along my lower lip. "I do work out, yes. Makes me feel good."

"Feel good. Right." I licked my lips nervously.

With a groan, Caleb leaned in and kissed me, his thumb tugging down on my chin so my mouth was open to the invasion of his tongue.

I looped my arms around the back of his neck, sliding my fingers into his hair.

Caleb slipped his hands under my ass and pulled me into his lap so I was straddling him—and his growing erection.

"Caleb?" I whispered the question against his lips.

It was a question he answered by gliding his hands up over my back and unsnapping my bra.

I trembled slightly, but did not resist when he pulled my straps down my arms, kissing along the path down one arm from my shoulder to my elbow.

"Shh, Jacey. I'm gonna take good care of you," Caleb murmured, pulling my bra from me completely and tossing it onto the nearby table. "We don't have to go all the way. Just stop me when you don't want to go any further."

"O-Okay," I said nervously. I hugged myself to him, my breasts rubbing against his chest, as I was embarrassed of my body.

Caleb didn't say anything. Instead, he laid me back on the bed so he was now on top of me, his dick hard against my mound. My legs widened of their own volition, accepting the press of his hips.

He leaned on one elbow, the air a bit cool where our bodies were separated. Namely, over my breasts.

I brought an arm up to cover myself, but Caleb kissed me and tugged my arm back down.

"Jacey, I want to see you. I want to see your beautiful breasts," Caleb said.

"I don't know about 'beautiful.'" I blushed.

Caleb stroked my cheek, then kissed me. "Let me be the judge of that."

With a sigh, I turned my face away to hide my insecurity and let Caleb look to his heart's content. What I heard was a sharp intake of breath.

Then I felt the rough pad of this thumb rub over my nipple as he cupped my breast.

My whole body jerked. It felt positively electric.

"Rose. I like it," Caleb murmured. "Damn, you're so beautiful, Jacey."

"Thanks," I said awkwardly, not sure what else to say. It was hard to believe the compliment, but the evidence of Caleb's straining cock was also hard to argue with.

Caleb turned my face back to him and kissed me thoroughly. "I mean it," he insisted. He must have heard the doubt in my voice.

I didn't know how to answer him, but then, Caleb didn't seem to need an answer. He kissed me again, then kissed my neck, drawing hard on the skin.

"Caleb?" I asked, wondering about the sharp sting, even as I tangled my fingers in his hair.

Caleb licked the spot. "I don't want any of those college boys thinking they can touch you. You're mine."

The idea sent a thrill down my spine. "I am?"

"Mhm. I've decided." Caleb nuzzled my neck. "Is that okay?"

"Y-Yeah," I said, my senses completely overwhelmed by the sight, smell, and feel of Caleb.

Caleb rocked his hips between my legs, and his cock rubbed right where I wanted it. I whimpered. "Good," Caleb whispered in my ear before starting back on the journey he'd embarked on.

He made his way slowly from my neck to my collarbone, then lower to my chest. I knew what was coming next, but still arched under him, pressing against his mouth when he sucked my nipple gently between his teeth.

It felt so good, I thought my brain might short-circuit.

I held Caleb's head to my breast, panting, getting warm and wet as he did positively indecent things with his tongue.

Then he let my nipple go with a low pop, and my body keenly felt the loss until he delivered the same attention to my other breast.

"Caleb," I all but whined, my hips rolling. I rubbed against his cock, and Caleb let out a hiss.

"I'll bet you're wet," he said. "Will you let me find out?"

"F-Find out? I can just tell you," I replied, confused. "I think I've soaked my panties." I figured I might as well tell him. He was going to feel it through his boxers soon enough.

Caleb chuckled. I felt his hand smooth down over my belly and play along the waistband of my bikini briefs. He skimmed a finger underneath, and I held my breath.

"Let me touch you, Jacey. Let me make you feel good," Caleb whispered.

"You're already making me feel good," I blurted, my body tingling deliciously under his touch.

"I can make you feel better," Caleb said, nipping my lower lip. "Let me?"

"W-What do you need me to do?" I asked.

"Relax, and spread your legs a little bit more," Caleb replied. His hand disappeared into my panties when I did what he asked.

Oh God. He was going to...

Caleb feathered his fingers over my slit, probably finding me very wet for him. Then he pushed past it, exploring me intimately.

His thumb found my clit and I jumped.

"Trust me," Caleb said against my skin. "Trust me, Jacey. I'm going to make you feel so good."

"I do trust you," I responded. "I'm just... it's so... it's so much!"

Caleb didn't reply, just rubbed the light stubble on his chin over my nipple while he thumbed my clit.

I thought I might come right out of my skin. "Caleb!"

Caleb sucked my nipple hard, pushing a finger inside me at the same time.

My virgin hole clamped around the invader.

"Relax. Shh, relax, Jacey." Caleb's words feathered over my wet, pearled nipple.

Panting, I thought relaxing thoughts. Though my body was uncertain, my mind trusted Caleb and wanted whatever he was about to give me.

When he deemed me relaxed enough, Caleb went back to his ministrations, sucking my nipples, rubbing his thumb against my clit. His finger began thrusting in me as well.

It was sensation overload, and I didn't want it to end.

I barely noticed when Caleb inserted a second finger. I had one hand buried in his hair, one digging into his back, and I was making sounds I didn't recognize.

Then Caleb hooked his fingers inside me, and I cried out, light exploding behind my eyes as the best orgasm I had EVER had rolled over my body.

Caleb pressed his forehead to mine as I came down, his expression strained. "You're not ready for full-on sex yet, are you?"

My brain was completely scrambled, and my breaths were coming in little gasps. I didn't know how to answer him.

"I didn't think so," he answered for himself. "I'm going to cum on your stomach, okay? You just lay still."

Breathless, I nodded.

Caleb sat back on his heels, pushing down his boxers just enough to get his cock out. I wasn't sure how cock size generally went, but in my eyes he was HUGE.

He wrapped his hand around his rigid shaft and started stroking himself, biting his lip, his head thrown back and his eyes closed.

I felt I should be helping, given all he'd done for me, so I sat up a little and tentatively reached out and touched his tip and the bead of precum that had formed there.

Caleb's eyes flew open, and he locked eyes with me.

"I want to help," I said softly.

Caleb swallowed and nodded. "Give me your hand."

I held it out to him, and he wrapped my hand around his swollen shaft. He kept his hand over mine, showing me how he liked to be jerked off.

It wasn't long before Caleb groaned, and his thick, white cum pulsed over my stomach. A little even landed on my breasts and chin.

Caleb's eyes became hooded, and he thumbed the little bit of cum off my chin. "Open your mouth."

I knew what he wanted, and I did exactly as I was told.

He pushed his thumb with his cum on it into my mouth. "Suck."

I licked his thumb and sucked it clean, surprised at the salty tang.

"Jesus FUCK that was hot," Caleb whispered.

"Yeah..." I agreed. "Yeah, it was..."

Caleb gave me a slow smile. "I'm going to go check out the drawers and see if I can't find something to clean you up with. Then, we're gonna snuggle."

"I'd like that," I said shyly. Though, I supposed I shouldn't be shy. I had Caleb's cum all over me.

Caleb slid off me and off the bed, and I missed his warmth almost immediately. He went through the few drawers there were next to the pantry, and came back triumphant with a towel.

Gently, Caleb wiped me clean of his cum, then tossed the towel aside and kissed me on the mouth. He climbed into the small bed and laid on his side, gathering me against him.

"What are we going to do when our parents find us?" I asked Caleb softly.

"Hope I'm not cock deep in you at the time," Caleb teased.

I swatted him. "I'm serious."

"Well, one, they'd actually have to find us, and it looks like that's going to be a while. Two, we'll be very discreet. I don't want to break my mother's heart, and I'd rather your father didn't kill me," Caleb said.

"I'd rather he didn't kill you, too," I responded.

"Are you staying on campus?" Caleb asked. "At the U?"

I giggled. "You really don't keep track, do you."

"What? Until yesterday, I was still fighting not to think about you at all," Caleb said defensively.

"How'd that work out for you?" I asked.

Caleb sighed and looked down at our near-naked bodies. "Not well. But now I'm not complaining."

"The semester started on the sixth. I live in Middlebrook in the Casa de Español so I can practice my Spanish. West Bank," I said.

"I hope it's not girls only," Caleb grinned.

I rolled my eyes. "It's not. But I do have a roommate."

"Does the sock on the door thing not work anymore?"

"Caleb!" I protested, blushing furiously.

Caleb kissed my temple. "Kidding, kidding. We'll work it out."

I bit my lip, staring out the window, outside our little bubble.

"I hope so," I said.

CHAPTER 11: HAPPY, HAPPY BIRTHDAY

-Jacey-

Caleb finally let me go to sleep after checking to make sure my pupils were evenly dilated. Since I'd been lucid in the hours following my head injury, Caleb had reluctantly decided my concussion, if I had one, wasn't that bad, and he'd continue to monitor me throughout my sleep.

My nearly-naked monitor was, however, snoring softly when I woke up. I bit my lip, holding back a laugh.

The moonlight was shining through the window, and I could see a million stars. I placed my hand on Caleb's cheek, and he blinked awake.

"You okay?" he asked muzzily. Then his gaze sharpened. "Ah, shit, I fell asleep!"

"Well, Dr. Killeen, I guess you're going to have to redo your residency," I admonished him with a straight face.

Mostly a straight face, anyway. I could feel the corners of my lips quirking up.

Caleb booped me on the nose. "You're a laugh and a half."

I pointed out the window. "Look at the sky."

We adjusted so Caleb could roll on his other side, me spooning him, and he looked out the window.

"Damn," he said in awe. "That's beautiful."

I wrapped my arm around his bare waist and laid my cheek against his. "This is one of the reasons I love coming up here. Everything about this place is beautiful."

Caleb took my hand and kissed the palm. "Especially the company."

"Hmm," I murmured, "that was a little cheesy, but I think I'll let it go."

Caleb laughed and twined his fingers with mine. "It's true. But yeah, I guess that was a bit cheesy."

We watched the sky for a while, then Caleb turned back to me so we were facing each other on our sides on the narrow bed. He reached out and stroked my cheek.

"Jacey," he whispered, pressing his lips to mine.

I'd never put my bra back on, so the only barriers between us were my bikini briefs and his boxers. The moonlight made Caleb's skin glow. It was almost unearthly, like looking at a live marble statue.

"Touch me again?" I begged when our lips parted. "Like you did before?" I felt more bold in the dark, and I ran my hands down over Caleb's chest.

Caleb wrapped my legs around his waist and rolled me underneath him. He kissed me with unhurried tenderness, his hips settling right where they belonged. I could feel him, hard again, straining for my core. It made me shiver.

"Cold?" he asked.

"N-No," I said. "Keep going, please."

"So polite," Caleb grinned against my lips. He put my palm right over his nipple. "Touch me, too."

I took his invitation, tentatively stroking his nipple, then rubbing it with my thumb the way he had mine. I could feel his cock swell more against my thigh and took that as a good sign.

Caleb, meanwhile, kissed his way down to the sensitive spot he'd made, drawing on it again. His hands massaged my breasts, and I moaned a little in the back of my throat.

"I'm going to take off your panties, Jacey," Caleb spoke softly against my breast. "That doesn't mean I'll do anything more than we already have. It just gives me better access."

"O-Okay," I agreed.

Caleb hooked his fingers into the waistband of my panties and peeled them down my thighs. He rubbed them through his fingers and grinned. "Wet already."

"It's kind of hard not to be. You're making me into a complete puddle," I replied with a blush.

"Good." Caleb tossed my panties the direction my bra had gone and pressed his hand over my mound, rubbing my clit with the butt of his palm.

"Oh my God, Caleb," I gasped as he latched onto one of my nipples and slid two fingers inside me. Then I winced.

Caleb noticed and his head came up. "Are you sore?"

I nodded. "A little bit. But... not so much I want to stop."

"Okay. Actually, let me try something else." Caleb gave my nipple a long, slow lick while he removed his fingers.

I furrowed my brow. "But I said it was good."

Caleb smiled against my skin as he kissed his way down over my belly. "This might be even better."

"What are you...?" I asked as Caleb prowled right off the end of the bed, kneeling on the floor. Then he put his hands under my knees and tugged so my ass was perched right over the end of the bed.

It wasn't until Caleb put my legs over his shoulders that I realized what he planned to do. "Caleb!"

"Shh, trust me. It's okay." Caleb put his mouth on my nether lips, delivering a kiss there before parting me open with his thumbs. "I'm going to taste you."

"C-Caleb..." I said uncertainly, not sure if I was going to taste good.

Caleb gave me a long, slow lick from my virgin hole to my clit. "Mmm..." he murmured.

I was shaking with anticipation, my whole body on fire for him. "Please, Caleb. Please."

He chuckled again, probably at my politeness, but did not leave me waiting. His clever tongue swirled up into me while he rubbed my clit with his nose.

I was so shocked by the sensation that I nearly bucked him off me, but Caleb held me down gently but firmly so he could eat me out at his own pace.

"Caleb..." I moaned, my hand fisting in his hair as my body began the first tremors of an orgasm. I didn't want him to stop. I never wanted him to stop.

When I came, I cried out his name again, rubbing myself against his face. I could feel him lapping up my juices, swallowing the evidence of my pleasure.

I was still trembling when Caleb stood, his cock straining in his boxers. There was even a small wet spot where the tip of him touched the cotton.

"Are you going to cum on my stomach again?" I asked as Caleb slipped his cock out of his boxer shorts.

"Yeah," Caleb said, standing over me with his cock in hand.

I swallowed, watching him stroke himself. Then I made a decision.

"Would you rather cum... inside me?" I whispered.

Caleb stilled. He squeezed his eyes shut. When he opened them again, there was a passion so raw in them that it struck me all the way to my core. And my core.

"Are you sure?" he rumbled.

I nodded and scooted back up the bed, holding his eyes, letting him see that I had no doubts.

Caleb prowled up after me. "It's gonna hurt a bit," he warned me.

"I kind of figured, what with that bat you're swinging," I joked nervously.

The intensity of Caleb's gaze made me stop laughing, though. "I'm a big man," he said. "You're not scared?"

"A little," I admitted. I held out my arms to him. "But I want my first time to be with you."

Caleb groaned and kissed me hard. He darted his tongue into my mouth, taking my mouth the way I knew he was about to take my body.

I trusted Caleb, though. I trusted him with everything I had, everything I was. He was a good man, a kind stepbrother, and a caring lover. I wanted him, and I wasn't going to change my mind.

While he kissed me forcefully, willing me to submit to him, his palm skimmed down over my belly and over my slit. He pressed two fingers into me, working them around carefully, scissoring them a bit.

It felt both good and uncomfortable at the same time. I suspected his cock would feel much the same inside me.

Despite the discomfort, I could feel myself getting wet for him again.

"That's it, baby," Caleb mumbled against my lips. "Let me get you all worked up. Just relax. I'm gonna take good care of you."

It was the first time he'd called me "baby." The pet name warmed my heart. "Am I your baby?" I whispered.

"Damn straight." Caleb curled his fingers inside me again, hitting just the right spot.

This time, when I came, Caleb lifted my thigh over his hip. I had just crested my orgasm and was coming back down when Caleb lined himself up with my entrance and pushed his tip inside me.

Just the tip was enough to make me gasp.

"Baby, relax. We've got a lot more to go. I want you to take all of me." Caleb began to slowly push himself deeper. "Shit, you're tight!"

An inch or two later, I felt him come up against resistance, and I whimpered at the burning sensation as he pushed.

Caleb took one of my hands and threaded his fingers through mine. "It's okay, baby. Breathe through it. I'm going to take care of that right now."

I wasn't quite sure how he intended to "take care" of it until he squeezed my hand and lunged, pushing the rest of himself in all at once.

There was a sharp pain, and I cried out, squeezing Caleb's hand. Tears filled my eyes and fell down my cheeks. It really hurt.

Caleb stayed still, not moving inside me. He wrapped his arms around me, one around my waist, the other cradling the back of my head. "Breathe, baby. Breathe. It's okay. It's okay. That part's over now."

I thought of begging Caleb to pull out, but when he tenderly kissed my tears, I decided I could stand it just this once. He needed this. I could feel his swollen need inside me.

"Is it—is it going to h-hurt like that if we keep going?" I still asked on a whimper. I wanted to be prepared, at least.

Caleb shook his head, holding me to him. "That's the worst it's ever going to feel. You're going to be sore if we keep going, and you'll be sore the next few times we have sex, but that goes away. I promise."

"Okay." I took a deep breath. "Go slow?"

"I will, baby." Caleb kissed me, then brought his hands down to my hips.

I felt his cock slowly slide out to the tip, then push back in. Again. And again. And again. Each time, he filled me to the hilt of him.

Caleb moved his thumb in to rub my clit while he moved inside me. My angry, raw core perked up a little at the sensation.

"Fuck me, you feel so good, Jacey," Caleb groaned. "You're so wet... so tight..."

I hugged my arms around Caleb's neck, burying my face in his shoulder. "I feel full," I mumbled into his skin, a bit embarrassed by this talk.

Caleb kissed my shoulder. "Baby, I need to go a little harder... I know you're sore. But bear with me, okay?"

"Okay." I clung to Caleb while he began thrusting sharply inside me. It hurt, but not nearly as much as when he'd torn past my hymen. I even felt a little bit aroused by what he was doing to my clit.

"Mmm, I'm close, baby. I-I'm gonna cum," Caleb groaned.

Much to my surprise, just as Caleb pushed deeper in me than he'd been before and released the first spurt of his hot cum in me, I also came. It wasn't a strong orgasm, but it was enough.

Caleb was still cumming when my little orgasm was over,

moaning into my hair. I could feel him jerking in me, filling me with his hot seed. I stroked his hair, holding him while he finished.

His cock went soft, or at least I thought it had. It went softer, anyway, not as swollen in me.

"What happens now?" I asked softly, still holding Caleb.

Caleb gave me a sweaty kiss. Then he looked up at the window and smiled. "Now we watch some shooting stars, I guess."

I looked past his shoulder, and sure enough, there were shooting stars streaking across the sky. "Oh wow," I whispered.

"Happy Birthday, Jacey," Caleb said, capturing my lips once more.

CHAPTER 12: HOLY FUCK

-Caleb-

I woke slowly, wondering if last night had been a dream. Then I saw Jocelyn, naked, sprawled across my chest, her braid half-undone, breathing deeply in sleep.

"Hey, baby," I whispered too softly to wake her. She needed her rest.

Her thigh was pressed between mine, rubbing against my already ready dick. Between morning wood and having this gorgeous creature enveloping my senses, I was harder than I'd ever been in my life. I was so hard it hurt.

Careful not to disturb her, I started giving myself some much-needed relief, fisting my hand up and down my shaft. When she woke up, we'd probably fuck again, but I needed release now.

I bit my lip against any sounds as I imagined it was Jocelyn's hand stroking my dick.

Precum began to bead, then trickle down over my fingers as I beat myself off, looking at Jocelyn's beautiful body.

Jocelyn stirred just as I was getting close. She winced when she moved, and I saw cum, a little pink with blood, trickle down her leg as she yawned and stood, stretching her arms over her head.

She looked down at me, and of course, saw me in the midst of jerking off. I felt my cheeks heat up.

"Good morning, beautiful," I said, giving her an apologetic half-smile. "I didn't want to wake you."

Jocelyn licked her lips, staring at my raging boner. "Good morning."

I knew exactly where I wanted those lips, but I wasn't sure she was ready for that yet. I started stroking myself again. "Nobody's found us yet. But I'm sure you know that."

"I kind of figured," Jocelyn replied, still staring at my dick.

"Morning wood," I finally explained. "Plus, there was this beautiful naked girl laying on top of me..."

Jocelyn blushed. "Can I help?" she asked softly.

My cock twitched. Oh, fuck, could she help. "Can you use your hand again?" I suggested eagerly.

Her tongue flicked out and licked her lips again. It was almost my undoing. "What if I put it in my mouth?"

Yep. This inquisitive girl was going to kill me. "I'd like that, but you don't have to."

"You had your tongue inside me. Seems I should return the favor," Jocelyn said, kneeling at the edge of the bed.

I wasn't going to say "no" to her offer. I sat up and put my knees on either side of her, presenting her with my aching cock. "I'm assuming you've never blown a guy before?"

Jocelyn shook her head.

"Right. No teeth. NO teeth, okay?" I instructed her. I took her hand and wrapped it around the base of my cock. "Take it slow. I'll tell you when I'm going to cum."

My eager student licked the precum that leaked over her fingers, then ran the flat of her tongue over my tip, catching the rest. I shuddered as she treated my cock like her own personal lollipop.

When she first took my tip in her mouth, I felt a little teeth, and I hissed.

Jocelyn looked up at me and winced. "Sorry," she said.

"It's okay," I replied. "Try again. NO teeth."

Jocelyn, more carefully this time, pushed her lips over my cock. I wound her ebony braid around my fist, trying to calm myself down while she sucked and licked me.

"Can you take me deeper?" I panted.

With a shrug, Jocelyn took me in a little bit more.

I used my grip on her hair to push myself further down her throat.

Jocelyn gagged and backed off, giving me a stern look. "Don't do that."

"S-Sorry," I said. "Just... trying to... help."

"Help yourself," Jocelyn grumped. "I'll suck you down as deep as I can, but don't choke me, okay?"

I nodded contritely. "Okay."

Jocelyn went down on my cock again, her cheeks puffing as she sucked me off.

Even with her fist around the base, some of my shaft wasn't in her hand or in her mouth, but I didn't want her to stop again. We could work on her depth later.

My balls tightened quickly, and I knew I was going to blow my load. I tugged on Jocelyn's hair. "Baby, I'm gonna cum."

To my surprise, Jocelyn didn't stop. She kept sucking, right up to when I came in her mouth and down her throat.

Jocelyn choked and coughed, cum dribbling out of her mouth as she pulled back. But then, she did the sexiest thing I'd seen her do yet. She swallowed.

"Shit," I wheezed, thumbing my cum off her chin. "Oh, baby, that was so HOT."

"Really?" Jocelyn asked, looking at me with those intelligent, yet innocent green eyes of hers.

A possessive sense of pride settled over me when I realized I was the only man who had ever touched her. I could tick the firsts off on my fingers. I got to give her tongue. I got to see her naked. I got to touch her breasts, finger her cunt. I'd taken her virginity. No man who came after me would ever have that from her.

The very idea of any man coming after me filled me with such rage that I had to set my teeth against a growl. Jocelyn Collins was MINE.

"Caleb?" Jocelyn inquired, looking nervous.

I realized I hadn't answered her question. I pulled her off balance and into my lap so she was clinging to my shoulders, her slit pressed right up against my still semi-hard cock. "The only thing hotter than that was when I had you last night under the stars."

Jocelyn blushed again. "I probably don't look as good in the cold light of day."

I raised my eyebrows and took her chin in my hand, forcing her to look at me. "You look perfect. You are perfect, Jacey. Perfect."

"I think you're perfect," Jocelyn responded, and planted a kiss on my lips.

Her kisses were so innocent, so full of the purest emotion that it made my heart hurt. I licked her lips, pushing my tongue into her mouth while I rubbed my cock back and forth along her slit.

Jocelyn moaned into my mouth when I tugged her nipple, anchoring one hand under her ass to keep her in my lap and almost riding my dick.

She soon started to get slick, and I felt her juices begin to coat my cock.

When we broke for air, Jocelyn looked at me, her brows pinched together. "You want it again, don't you. You want to... be inside me."

"Hell yes," I agreed. I poked the furrow between her eyebrows. "But you're not sure."

"I'm still sore," Jocelyn said softly. "Like, really sore. But you're also making me wet, so..."

"Bodies can be confusing sometimes." I kissed her nose and gave up the idea of dipping my dick in her. "Mind if we do something else?"

"Do you want me to give you another blowjob?" Jocelyn asked.

God, she was adorable. "I'll never say 'no' to a blowjob, Jocelyn. I'm a red-blooded man. I was thinking something else, though."

"You want me to jerk you off?" Jocelyn tried again.

I kissed her to stop her guessing, even though it was cute. "I want to titty-fuck you."

Jocelyn blinked. "'Titty-fuck'?"

"You push your boobs together, I pump my dick between them, and pretty soon I cum on your face," I explained.

"And that'll be okay instead of sex?" Jocelyn asked.

I gave her a slow grin. "While I'd rather be cock deep in you any day of the week, like you said, you're sore. Yes, I will enjoy titty-fucking you very much." I leaned up close to her ear. "Then I think you need me to go down on you again. Don't you. Kiss it and make it better."

Jocelyn's breath hitched.

"I thought so," I murmured. I laid Jocelyn down on the bed, settling myself down on her stomach. "This okay? Not too heavy?"

"It's okay," Jocelyn replied, looking up at me with wide, trusting eyes.

"Push those big boobs of yours together, baby," I said, laying a hand on her cheek.

Jocelyn pushed her breasts together.

I showed her how to adjust her hold so there would be a tight little hole for me to thrust into between her breasts and her sternum.

"Remember, I'm cumming on your face. Don't be too surprised. And keep those breasts together tight." I gripped her upper arms, then thrust my cock between her breasts, my dick still slick from rubbing against her slit.

Jocelyn held her breasts tightly in place, watching the head of my dick appear and disappear between her breasts.

"Mmm... Jesus fuck, baby... this feels so good..." I muttered, my precum starting to dribble onto her collarbone.

I nearly lost it when her tongue flitted out to lick the head of my cock on a down stroke.

"Baby, I'm cumming, close your eyes," I groaned just as I began to jettison cum.

Jocelyn squeezed her eyes shut, and I kept thrusting, getting my cum everywhere from her breasts to her hairline.

When I finished, I reached down and wiped the cum from her eyelids. "You can open your eyes now."

Jocelyn looked up at me and smiled. "You enjoyed that?"

"Like you have to ask," I snorted. I eased myself out from between Jocelyn's breasts, and she released them, letting them bounce to the sides once more.

I could tell Jocelyn was proud of the good job she'd done, getting me off. She had every reason to be. I was now a deeply sated man. "Let me get a towel. Much as I like seeing you covered in my cum, I think it'd be best if we clean up a little bit before I go down on you."

"Okay." Jocelyn sat up on her elbows while I went to get another towel. Carefully, I dabbed my cum off of her, using the opportunity to check out her bruised cut as well.

Jocelyn curled her hand around my wrist. "I'm fine, Caleb."

I smiled at her and gave her a kiss that promised more.

Jocelyn kissed me back, her fingers spiking through my hair.

"Mmm... baby, let me make you come," I whispered against her lips. "I could honestly do this all day and all night, but I promised you an orgasm."

Jocelyn giggled and gave me one last peck on the lips before lying back on the bed, her head on one arm.

I got off the bed and knelt beside it, rather than at the foot this time. Jocelyn understood and turned herself around.

Her head bumped the wall and she frowned.

I grinned and grabbed the pillow, tucking it behind her head so her head was propped up against the wall. "I didn't want you to miss the show."

The bed was narrow, so Jocelyn was already hanging a bit off the edge. I got between her legs and put her knees over my shoulders.

Then I gave her slit a long, slow lick.

"Caleb..." Jocelyn looked down at me with those wide green eyes of hers.

There was nothing I liked more than seeing those eyes blissed out with pleasure. With a wink, I sucked her clit, lapping it with my tongue.

Jocelyn made a little noise in her throat, helpless under my ministrations.

I kept going, tasting her slowly. She still tasted faintly of last evening's activities, but also musky, that irresistible taste that was uniquely Jocelyn.

"Caleb," Jocelyn moaned, her legs straining over my shoulders.

I licked her inside and out until she was begging, then began darting my tongue in and out of her, rubbing her clit with my nose.

Jocelyn reached out and gripped my hair almost painfully, gasping and holding me against her cunt. I massaged her thighs, breathing sparingly as I pleasured her.

Finally, Jocelyn's juices coated my face in a rush as she came hard, her inner muscles tensing around my tongue.

I licked and swallowed every drop, locking eyes with her heavy-lidded ones. She was completely blissed out.

I smiled against her, delivering a kiss to her slit, then stood up and got the towel to wipe my face.

"B-Bath?" Jocelyn chattered after a moment.

"Bath?" I repeated. I looked down at her and grinned. "Yeah, might as well. But I'd suggest we put our underwear back on, just in case somebody DOES find us while we're out there."

"Good plan," Jocelyn agreed. She scooted down the bed and was a bit wobbly when she got to her feet.

I smirked. I'd done that. "Put on your boots, too. I might not have footwear, but that doesn't mean you have to go without."

Jocelyn cupped my cheek and kissed me.

I wrapped her in my arms, holding her naked body against mine. It was going to be a damn shame to cover up those beautiful breasts of hers.

After a long moment, I finally broke our hug and gave Jocelyn a kiss on the nose. "Okay. Off to get clean."

As Jocelyn shimmied back into her bra and panties, I knew one thing for certain.

My body might get clean today, but my mind was going to be filled with dirty images of Jocelyn for the rest of my life.

CHAPTER 13: THE BUBBLE BURSTS

~~~~~~

-Jacey-

Caleb and I made our way back to the shore. Sure enough, our clothes and lifejackets were gone. But at least there was no bear.

Since I was the one wearing boots, I picked a careful path through the rocks, leading Caleb deep enough into the water that we could both rinse off a bit.

I'd had Caleb's cum EVERYWHERE on my body, and even though Caleb was always sweet to me after and cleaned me up with a towel, I still felt the need to let some water run over me.

Sitting waist deep in the water on an obliging boulder, I cupped my hands together and trickled water over my hair. It was coming out of its braid, and I had no idea what I was going to do without a comb or a brush. If I couldn't tame it, I was going to look like a swamp witch coming out of the bog with sticks and leaves in her tangled hair.

As though he heard me, Caleb moved to sit behind me, pulling me into his lap. Even now, he was hard for me.

Me.

It was like I'd been given this mysterious power over him, and I was relishing in it.

Caleb took out my hair band and carefully undid my hair, combing his fingers through it with care. "God, your hair is beautiful. And so soft..."

I felt myself blushing. "You won't think that if it stays unbraided. I'll look like a hermit who just wandered out of her cave."

Caleb chuckled and kissed my neck. "I'll braid it for you."

"Really?" I looked back at him. "You know how to do that?"

"Sure. My dad used to do it for my mom. He showed me," Caleb said.

"That sounds really nice," I replied softly. I knew Caleb missed his father. I wished he got along better with mine, but I could understand the complex animosity between them.

Caleb cupped more water over my hair, rinsing it out. He gently detangled any snarls with his fingers, then slowly braided it back up, finishing up by wrapping the hair binder around the bottom.

"Thanks," I murmured, looking up at him. Then I saw a mischievous glint in his blue eyes. "What? What are you—"

Caleb's answer was to slide his hand into my panties, washing me out himself.

I gasped and gripped his thighs. "Caleb!"

"What?" he asked innocently. "Have to get you nice and clean."

"Nice and clean" apparently meant pushing his fingers into me as well. I dug my nails into his thighs and moaned.

"Yeah, I think a bath was a great idea," Caleb whispered in my ear, nibbling along the shell.

There wasn't a person or boat in sight. I wasn't sure my oversexed body would have cared in the slightest if there was.

"Come for me, baby," Caleb said, adding his thumb on my clit to the mix. "I know you want to."

Of course, I wanted to. I wanted anything my stepbrother wanted to give me. Except, perhaps, full on sex. At least for a while. I was still sore around his fingers as he hooked them inside me.

"Caleb!" I cried as he wrought another orgasm from me.

"Good girl," Caleb responded, kissing and nipping along my neck and shoulder. He unsnapped my bra and massaged his wet hands underneath, "rinsing" my chest.

"You just want to play with my breasts," I accused him.

"Absolutely," Caleb replied unrepentantly. He rubbed circles with his thumbs over my nipples.

My eyelids fluttered. "Caleb."

"Yeah, beautiful?" Caleb nuzzled my shoulder.

"It feels... so good... when you touch me," I confessed.

I felt Caleb's lips curve up in a smile against my skin. "I like it when you touch me, too."

"Is that an invitation?" I asked, giving Caleb a wicked grin.

"Well, you know, my dick is very, very dirty..." Caleb feigned innocence.

I laughed. "You're a bad, bad man." But I did carefully turn and brace my boots against a lower rock. They were getting flooded with water, but there was no helping that, and they were rubber, so they would dry anyway.

I slipped my hand into his boxers under the water and took out his cock. It wasn't as hard as it usually would be, but I blamed the cold water. It sure perked up when I started stroking it.

"Mmm, yeah, baby. Just like that," Caleb groaned.

In an inspired moment, I pulled the front of my bra down with my free hand until my breasts popped out the top, letting him look his fill while I jerked him off.

Caleb stared and panted. His hand curled around mine, encouraging me to go faster and squeeze just a little bit tighter.

Soon enough, his milky white cum swirled into the water as he let out a grunt of satisfaction.

"Oh, baby," Caleb sighed as I readjusted my bra over my breasts. "You're amazing, Jacey."

I smiled and gave him a kiss. "Just returning the favor."

Caleb tucked himself back into his boxers. "I think maybe we should go back to the cabin and eat."

My stomach growled, and I blushed while Caleb laughed.

"Guess somebody agrees with me," he said, rubbing my belly. He playfully poked his finger into my belly button.

I started picking my way back over the rocks, navigating for the smoothest ones, shaking my head, letting Caleb hang onto my shoulders. He was pretty good at finding a safe path himself, carefully working his way back to the shore with me.

Once we got to shore, I dumped water out of my boots and put them back on. Caleb's angry legs were looking a little better, especially his shins, which had gotten the worst of it.

We made our way back to the cabin. There'd still been no signs of life all day.

Or so we thought.

The first sound I heard as we neared the cabin was a strange click.

Caleb's eyes widened and he quickly pushed me behind him.

"You little shits been messin' around in my cabin, eatin' my food?!" the voice of an older man carried through the front door.

I saw it was ajar and there was the barrel of a shotgun pointed at us through the opening.

"Yes, sir," Caleb said. "We got lost in the storm and we needed shelter—"

"Get the FUCK off my property!" the older man howled.

Caleb frowned. "Sir, as I understand it, this property belongs to the Canadian government..."

The ground in front of Caleb exploded. I clamped my hands over my mouth to stifle a shriek.

"What are you, a Mountie? Get the FUCK out of here!" the man yelled.

"All right," Caleb said after a moment of silence. "If you could please direct us to the nearest road—"

"Find yer own damn road," the old man shouted and spat on the ground outside the door.

"Caleb..." I whispered.

Caleb took my hand and squeezed it. "Fine then. We'll be on our way." He backed away, heading further into the woods, holding me behind him.

"Say, that a woman?" the older man called once Caleb finally turned around and started leading me God only knew where.

Caleb stiffened. "That's none of your damn business."

The shotgun cocked again. "I think it is. I think maybe I'm owed some payment for my hospitality."

"Jacey," Caleb said, leaning down by my ear. "Run."

"Caleb—!"

"RUN!" Caleb repeated, giving me a shove.

I ran as fast as my boots would take me, hearing a gunshot behind me. I stopped and turned, but even though they were spindly, the trees were too thick for me to see what had happened.

"Caleb?" I called behind me.

When he didn't appear, I started back the direction I came. Or at least I thought I did. But it turned out I had no idea where I'd gone, or how to get back to where I'd come from.

"Caleb?" I called again, weaving through the trees over beds of pine needles, moss, and dirt.

Someone grabbed my shoulder and I spun around.

An older man I didn't recognize wearing a flannel shirt and carrying a shotgun gave me a yellow-teethed smile. "Well hello there, darlin'. I'm afraid Caleb can't make it. But aren't you a pretty thing..."

I backed up, but there wasn't far to go before my back was to the scratchy bark of one of the spindly pine trees. "What do you want? Where's Caleb?"

The man made eye contact with my boobs, then looked back up at me with a lascivious grin. "I think we can figure something out, don't you?"

"S-Stay away from me," I said.

"Not to worry, darlin'. I know how to show a girl a good time," the older man responded, reaching out and trailing a dirty finger along my jaw.

I jerked my head away and squeezed my eyes shut. "Please just go away."

The older man laughed. Then there was a crunching noise, and the laughter stopped abruptly.

I peeked one eye open and saw Caleb, bleeding from his temple, standing over the old man, who was now on the ground. Caleb was holding a bloody rock in his hand.

"Caleb!" I ran forward and wrapped my arms around him. "Caleb, I was so scared! What happened? You're bleeding!"

Caleb dropped the rock and held me tightly, his chest rising and falling rapidly. "It just grazed me. It knocked me over for a bit, but... I really think he planned to kill me."

I looked down at the older man on the forest floor. His eyes were wide and sightless, and his skull was dented in. It didn't take a medical degree to determine this guy was dead.

"It's okay, Caleb," I said, noting my stepbrother was also staring at the man with wide eyes. "It's okay. You had to. He was going to hurt me." I stroked his back, hanging onto him tightly.

Caleb swallowed and turned his face away. "Let's just go, Jacey. He came from somewhere, so there must be a road near here."

I nodded vigorously and took Caleb's hand, tugging him away from the grisly scene. "Yes, let's go. Let's just get out of here. You never know if he was expecting company, and if they're anything like him, we don't want to meet them."

"Right," Caleb said. He hesitated then picked up the gun with his free hand and let me lead him away.

We walked in silence for several minutes.

"Caleb, he really was going to hurt me," I finally whispered.

Caleb dropped his hand from mine, only to slide his arm around my shoulders. "I know. I... I couldn't let that happen to you."

The blood from his temple had dried in rivulets down his cheek. I wanted to get Caleb to civilization to get him to a doctor. Of course, with my head injury, he probably wanted the same for me.

"I can't believe no one came to that part of the lake in two days," I observed.

"It's probably the rocks." Caleb squeezed my shoulder. "I'm okay, Jacey. You don't have to worry."

I looked up at him. "I'm going to worry anyway. I know what you did isn't easy, and you got shot at and your shins and everything... plus you don't have shoes and we're going over all these pine needles."

"I'm getting used to it," Caleb said manfully.

With a sigh, I leaned up and kissed his cheek. "We'll talk about it later, I guess. I don't want to upset you, but I want you to know I'm listening."

Caleb bumped his hip against mine, and that was how I knew we were going to be okay.

We found a clearing eventually with some scrubby grass. Neither of us knew much about edible plants or berries, so we left things alone even though we were starving. Mostly, we were thirsty. I wished we'd had the good sense to take some things from the cabin before leaving it this morning.

I sat on the ground, and Caleb laid down with his head in my lap. Despite what he'd said, he still looked troubled. I combed my fingers through his hair and hummed for him.

"We shouldn't rest long. We should try to find shelter, or the road, while it's still daylight," Caleb murmured, his eyes heavy.

"Mhm," I replied softly, still carding his hair. "We'll rest just a little bit."

Caleb's eyes fluttered closed, and I was careful not to jostle him while he slept.

I was beginning to doubt this road existed, but the man had to have come from somewhere.

Then I heard a rumbling not far off, and my eyes widened.

"Caleb!" I shook his shoulder. "Caleb!"

"Snrk?" Caleb came around, but was still groggy.

"It's a logging truck!" I said.

CHAPTER 14: FROM BAD TO WORSE

-Caleb-

I sat up from Jocelyn's lap, listening as she was. Sure enough, there was a familiar rumbling sound, the same sound we'd heard when we pulled off the road coming to the lake for one of the big bastards to pass.

"Come on," I said, getting to my feet. I'd been lying there, trying to forget what I'd done, trying to unsee the blood and the dented skull. I'd also been trying not to lose hope as Jocelyn and I made our way aimlessly through the forest.

But now there was hope in the form of a large truck.

I pulled Jocelyn up next to me and started walking in the direction of the sound. Even if we missed the truck—and considering how they zoomed along, we probably would—we would at least be able to find the road and wait for the next one.

Even if I ended up going to some Canadian prison for the rest of my life, I wanted to get Jocelyn to food, shelter, water, and, God willing, a hospital.

Pine needles pricked my feet as we walked, but I decided to call it a small penance for killing a man. I was sure my true penance would come later.

M. FRANCIS HASTINGS

"It's not far," Jocelyn said. "I know it's not."

"No, I don't think it is, either," I agreed. I held her hand tightly. My world felt as though it was spinning out of control, and she was gravity. My only anchor in the storm.

Road dust in the trees was our first clue. The logging truck had pulled quite a cloud behind it. But we fought our way through and found the gravel road.

"You can't possibly walk on this," Jocelyn observed, looking at my feet.

"Probably not," I agreed. "But we can follow alongside the road in the woods."

Jocelyn nodded. "Good plan. Which direction, though?"

I looked down one way, then the other. "Christ, I don't know. Right?"

"Yeah. Either we hit a logging camp or the main road. We'll get help no matter where we end up," Jocelyn decided.

She and I started down the side of the road, still nearly naked, like Adam and Eve coming out of the woods. I wondered if we'd find the dead man's vehicle stashed somewhere. Maybe he'd have left his keys.

I didn't see a vehicle along the road, but after a curve in the road, we did see a logging camp.

Stripped pine tree trunks were being loaded onto a long, chain-covered trailer. There was a building that was clearly the office, then a few scattered cabins around that, which I imagined housed the workers themselves.

"We made it!" Jocelyn said excitedly, bouncing on the balls of her feet.

I put a hand on her shoulder to stop her bouncing. It was making her boobs bounce with her, and I didn't like the idea of her, even so innocently, putting on a show for other men. Jocelyn was MINE.

When we got close to the camp, a whistle went up, and the loading stopped with one log dangling on a chain in the air over the truck.

"What have we got here?" a guy in overalls asked, marching down the road toward us.

"Hello, sir," Jocelyn said. "We had a boating accident during the storm the other day and we're terribly lost. Could we possibly use... um... do you have like a phone that actually works up here or some way we could contact the authorities to come get us?"

The guy in overalls scratched his chin, looking at Jocelyn speculatively. I didn't like it. "American?"

"Yes, sir," Jocelyn said. "I'm Jacey, this is my stepbrother, Caleb."

"Had to be American. Nobody else would walk around near naked in the Canadian woods," the guy chuckled. "I'm Girard. Afraid we don't have any working phone around here."

"Who do you call in case of an emergency?" I asked, stepping in front of Jocelyn.

"We've got trucks. We drive to a hospital," Girard said as though I was stupid.

"Could we get a ride to the nearest hospital, please?" Jocelyn piped up, peering over my shoulder. She was shooting me confused looks.

I knew I'd confused her, but I had a bad feeling in my gut. "Or maybe tell us how far to the main road?"

"You're not walking to the main road barefoot, son. I'm surprised you made it here from the lake," Girard said. "As for a ride, well, that's complicated."

Jocelyn swallowed, her throat undulating against my shoulder. I reached back and took her hand in mine.

"Why is it complicated? If you're looking for a reward, I'm sure you can make some sort of arrangement with my stepdad or my mom," I replied.

Girard sucked his teeth, rocking on the heels of his steel-toed boots. "Well, you see, son, this here is an illegal logging operation."

"Oh crap," Jocelyn whispered.

I squeezed her hand tighter. "That's no business of ours. We just want to get to a hospital."

"I'll bet you do. You two look pretty banged up. But now you know we're back here, well, that creates problems for us," Girard said.

"Caleb?" Jocelyn breathed next to my ear, the stress in her voice having ratcheted up almost as high as the pounding in my blood.

"Sir, I promise you, we're going to forget all about it. We just need a way out of here. Hell, we don't even know where we are anymore," I tried reasoning with him.

Girard shrugged. "Afraid that isn't going to work for us, son." He let out a high-pitched whistle.

The other men back in the encampment started stalking toward us.

"Oh God. Oh God," Jocelyn said.

I knew her eyes were darting around, just like mine, trying to find some way out of this. "Um... thank you for your time. We'll just be going, then." I didn't even have to tell Jocelyn to run.

It wasn't much use, though. Jocelyn was wearing clunky, awkward wading boots while I was barefoot. The combination did not make for speed for either one of us. Whereas our pursuers were wearing steel-toed, rugged terrain footwear.

We made it about half a mile before two men tackled me to the forest floor and Girard snatched Jocelyn by her hair.

"Jacey!" I called, panicking.

"I'd be worrying more about yourself," one of my attackers said.

I struggled. I was in good shape and worked hard to keep myself that way, but there were two burly lumberjacks holding me down. I wasn't exactly equal to that.

Still, when they hauled me to my feet and Girard marched Jocelyn past me, I bared my teeth at him. "If you harm one hair on her head..."

"You'll what? Threaten me to death? I'm shaking in my boots," Girard deadpanned.

"We'll have to go back and make sure they didn't leave a trail. There're probably people looking for them," one of the other lumberjacks said.

Girard nodded. "Come on, let's get these two locked up until we decide what to do with them."

"If they were around Little Wiikaa, Bill will know," the two lumberjacks who went back into the woods said to each other.

Jocelyn looked at me. We had a pretty good idea of who "Bill" was. The question was, what would these men do when they discovered Bill?

We were half-marched, half-dragged to a windowless shed and thrown inside on the rough plank floor. The door slammed shut, but light still came in faintly through cracks between the wallboards and around the door.

I reached out for Jocelyn, my hand finally landing on her shoulder. She crawled immediately into my lap and hugged me.

"We have to get out of here before they find him," she said, voicing my own thoughts.

"I know." I let my eyes adjust to the low light of the shed then began looking and feeling around. There was nothing in here of consequence, just things that they wouldn't want to get wet—extra blankets and clothes—as well as other supplies we might have even kept under our tarp, such as bottled water. The most dangerous item in the shed was a butterknife someone had left in a half-eaten loaf of bread.

Jocelyn, meanwhile, was exploring the back of the shed, pushing her booted feet experimentally against the boards. "I think we might be able to kick them and break them," she whispered to me. "But I didn't get a good look at what's on the other side, and I'm afraid they'll hear us."

"We'll have to wait for night, then, or for another opportunity to present itself," I sighed, raking a hand over my hair. "In the meantime, let's eat something, drink some water, and rest a bit. It'll be a couple of hours before they find Bill."

"I wish they'd start sawing again," Jocelyn muttered, cutting me off a hunk of bread and handing me a water bottle.

The bread turned out to be a sweet bread and really good. We finished off the loaf, sitting on a blanket I spread on the floor and swigging water.

I laid down after we'd set the bottles aside and motioned for Jocelyn to lay with me. She pillowed her head on my bicep and snuggled into me, her arm across my stomach. I played idly with her braid, thinking of what we could possibly do next to aid in our escape.

Jocelyn, thank God, drifted off into a light sleep. I kissed her forehead, wracking my brain for some way to protect her. To get her out of here.

I must not have noticed myself drifting off as well, because the next thing I knew, the door was rattling and my eyes were flying open. I quickly grabbed another blanket and wrapped it around Jocelyn, who came awake with a start.

"Shh," I whispered, looking at the long shadows of light along the floor. Hours had passed. Had they found Bill?

Girard poked his head in the shed, took a look around, and chuckled. "Made yourselves right at home, I see."

"Please, let us go," Jocelyn said, tucking the blanket high up under her chin to hide her mostly-naked body.

"Well, about that. My men just radioed me with some interesting news. Seems old Bill is sitting in the forest, not far from his cabin, with his head bashed in. Now, I know it was a bit early for moose-hunting season, but I don't think the Canadian Forest Service is giving out corporal punishment for breaking that law." Girard raised an eyebrow at us. "Care to explain?"

"We don't know this Bill person," Jocelyn replied quickly, while I just kept my mouth shut.

"Really? Because there were bare footprints and some woman's size boot prints near his body," Girard pressed. "Care to revise that lie of yours?"

Jocelyn squished closer to me, practically mummified in the blanket, and gave Girard a harsh look. "What are you, CSIs now?"

Girard stepped into the shed, his gaze cold. I looked past him. There were at least five men behind him, looking equally stoic. "Bill was a friend."

"Bill was a pervert!" Jocelyn insisted. She struggled her arms out of the blanket and grabbed for me when I stood to face Girard down.

"I killed him." I let the truth marinate around him for a while, then continued, "He was trying to hurt my stepsister."

"Ah." Girard gave Jocelyn a long once-over. "Well, can't blame the man. That body's made for sin."

Jocelyn pulled the blanket back up to cover herself.

"I don't care what you think her body's made for. She's my stepsister, and I won't have ANYONE messing with her," I said. I wasn't going down without a fight. If it came to it, I was taking some of these bastards with me if they decided to go for Jocelyn. Or I'd die trying.

Girard chuckled. "Oh, you've been a very bad boy, Caleb."

"So now you know I murdered somebody and we know about your logging operation. Does that make us even enough for you to let us go?" I demanded.

Girard stroked his chin. "I'll have to think about that." He walked back toward the door, then turned around and winked. "Don't go anywhere."

His laughter carried through the ill-fitted boards as the door slammed behind him.

CHAPTER 15: DARK DECISIONS

-JACEY-

In the last light of the day, Caleb and I ransacked the clothes in the shed, finally finding pants and shirts that fit both of us. There were even socks, and a pair of boots for Caleb. Unfortunately, none of the steel-toed boots in the shed were small enough for me. I was left with my rubber, knee-high waders.

The pants were also far too long on me, so I tucked them inside my wading boots. I had found a T-shirt that fit me, though it was tight over the chest, and a flannel button-down to go over it.

Caleb was dressed similarly, only his button-down was blue instead of red.

When night fully fell, Caleb and I moved to the back of the shed. Caleb put a blanket up against the back wall, and we started kicking the boards, letting the quilt muffle our efforts.

My head snapped around when I heard the door open, and I winced as a flashlight shone in my eyes.

Even though I couldn't yet see it, I heard the distinctive cock of a gun.

"I'd thank you kindly not to ruin our shed," a man I didn't recognize said flatly.

"S-Sorry," I stuttered.

The barrel of the gun sparkled in the light of the flashlight as he pointed the gun first at Caleb, then at me, then back at Caleb. "If I have to come back in here, one of you is getting shot."

"Yes, sir," I gulped.

"Good girl. Caleb?" the man prompted.

Caleb was quiet for a beat longer than I thought was prudent, but then he finally said, "Fine."

"Good. Now, both of you get some sleep. Pretty sure Girard's going to decide what to do with you in the morning," the man said. He swung the door shut.

I heard the chain and padlock again.

Hopeless, I flopped cross-legged on our blanket. "Caleb," I whispered, "are we going to die?"

Caleb was silent a long time. Then he sat down next to me and pulled me into his arms. "I don't know, Jacey."

I choked back a sob. I didn't want to give that asshole outside the satisfaction of hearing me blubber.

Caleb kissed my temple, then my lips, trying to comfort me.

I wrapped my arms around his neck and kissed him back, playing with his hair.

With a low groan, Caleb pulled back a bit. "Jacey," he murmured in my ear, "if... if this is going to be our last night..."

I knew what he wanted. I wanted it, too. If we were going to die, I wanted to be close with him at least one more time.

I shrugged out of my flannel shirt and felt in the dark for his, undoing the buttons and sliding it down over his shoulders.

Caleb put a hand on my waist and massaged my skin with his thumb, seeking out my mouth once more and kissing me more urgently.

I started reaching to peel off my T-shirt, but Caleb caught my hand and twined his fingers through mine.

"Just push it up, with your bra. If they come barging in, I want you to be able to get clothes back on quickly," Caleb said.

"Okay." I pushed my shirt and bra up.

Caleb's hand felt its way up my bare skin and landed on one of my breasts. He massaged it, thumbing my nipple.

I made a sound in my throat, but Caleb quickly kissed me again, muffling any more sounds.

Caleb laid me down gently then opened my pants and slid them down just far enough so that I could spread my knees for him. "Baby..." he murmured, teasing his fingers up inside me, "I know you're probably still a bit sore, and FUCK you're tight..."

I bit my lip against making noise and laid a hand on his cheek. "It's okay. I want you to."

In the dark, I heard Caleb's zipper open while his fingers worked magic inside me. He pressed his lips to mine as I started making desperate little sounds in my throat.

"That's it, baby," he whispered. "Come for me. Come around my fingers."

He found that special spot again, and just barely managed to crash his lips over mine before I let out a yowl, shuddering underneath him as my orgasm rushed through me.

Caleb slowly withdrew his fingers. I soon felt the thick head of his cock pressing against my entrance.

"Relax, baby," Caleb murmured, stroking my hair with one hand while his other arm circled underneath my hips, pulling them up while he gently pushed.

It was much easier than the first time, but he was still so big it was a bit uncomfortable. I whimpered as he inched inside me.

"You're doing so good, baby," Caleb said, kissing me and running his hand over my breast, teasing my nipple. "Relax for me... I'm only about half in."

Half?! I was glad he couldn't see my eyes bulging out of my head at that revelation. Indeed, the inches didn't seem to stop. When he hit a sore spot, and I let out a little gasp, he'd pull back a little, then push back in a few times until my body relaxed enough for him to keep going.

The last couple of inches, Caleb reached down to massage my clit while he sank into me, distracting me from the discomfort.

"Are you okay, baby?" he asked, his voice strained with the effort to hold himself back.

I nodded against his cheek, not trusting myself to speak. It hurt a bit, still, but it was nothing like the first time. This time it was... okay. Tolerable.

Caleb began easing himself out, only to surge back in.

I gasped as his large cock filled me again to the brim.

We both realized at the same time I was going to be absolutely unable to be quiet, so Caleb kissed me and kept his mouth on mine, swallowing every sound I made while he made slow love to me.

As the sex progressed, Caleb inevitably became more swollen inside me, but I was slick enough that his entry was still rather easy.

His thrusts became sharper, and I realized it had stopped hurting. In fact, I was starting to tingle inside.

"Caleb?" I whispered, a little confused by the change.

Caleb smiled against my lips and started worrying my clit in earnest.

I didn't know what to make of the building sensations. And then it didn't matter. I didn't care. I felt bliss crackling through my whole body, and I didn't need or want an explanation. I just didn't want it to stop.

"There's my baby," Caleb groaned, thrusting harder and faster still.

I dug my nails into his T-shirt-covered back crying out into his mouth as my inner muscles trembled and then fisted around his cock.

Caleb moaned back into my mouth, and I felt him cum, spurting hot inside me.

We held each other a long time, Caleb on top of and inside me as he softened.

"How did that feel?" Caleb asked, but I could feel his smirk against my lips.

"Pretty proud of yourself, aren't you," I grinned back.

"Shouldn't I be?" Caleb chuckled smugly.

I kissed him. "You have every right to be. That felt sooo good."

"Good." Caleb reluctantly pulled out of me. He got us back into our clothes, though neither of us put the flannel shirts back on. We'd created too much heat between us.

Caleb wrapped his arms around me and laid down on his back, encouraging me to lay my head on his chest.

I draped my arm over his waist, listening to his heartbeat and the sound of his breath, which gently stirred wisps of my hair.

Caleb rubbed the back of my neck.

A thousand words I could say swirled in my mind as silence fell between us.

"What are you thinking about?" Caleb asked softly.

I shrugged. "Lots of things. Things I shouldn't think about and don't need to worry about. Things I'm worried about anyway."

"I'm going to do everything I can to make sure that we don't die," Caleb said, toying with my braid.

"I know. Me, too," I replied.

His lips brushed the top of my head. "What else are you thinking about?"

"Stuff. Weird stuff." I furrowed my brow. "I don't know."

"You can tell me," Caleb said.

"Well, you know, I wonder if this is wrong sometimes..." I responded slowly, glad he couldn't see my blush in the dark.

Caleb cupped my ass, pulling me against him so I was half-riding his thigh. "Does it feel wrong?"

"No, it feels... good," I whispered. "Every time you touch me... it feels... right."

"Me, too," Caleb said. "I'm glad I was your first. I... fuck... God help me... I want to be your last."

I winced. "If things go the way they're going, that might not be difficult."

Caleb's arms tightened around me. "Don't think that way. We'll figure this out. We're not going to die. I refuse. Now that I have you, I refuse to lose you."

I snuggled Caleb, not sure what to say to that. They were desperate words without any hope of being a promise, but I knew he was just trying to keep my spirits up. I knew he must be scared shitless, just like me.

"What else is bothering you?" Caleb asked after a moment.

I bit my lip. "Well, if we do get out of this and we do get rescued, what do we tell Jeanie and Dad?"

Caleb's fingers stilled in my hair. "Nothing. We tell them nothing. My mom already said she thought it was gross, and I'm pretty sure Hank will kill me."

"And me," I said. "I'm pretty sure he was hanging onto the whole 'virgin until marriage' thing."

"Knowing your dad, that's a hill he was probably willing to die on," Caleb snorted. "Then again, I like that about conservative fathers. They don't ask questions about that."

"True," I replied. Not wanting to keep answering Caleb's questions, I let my hand wander down over his toned stomach to slide into the waistband of his pants.

Caleb caught my wrist. "Nice try. But there's something big that's bothering you, and you're not telling me."

"Aside from certain death?" I said sheepishly.

Caleb clucked his tongue. "I'm more than happy for you to stroke my dick, don't get me wrong. But I want us to finish our conversation first."

I sighed. "We've been doing it... without a condom."

Caleb's breath caught. "True."

"I'm not on anything," I murmured.

With a sigh of his own, Caleb cupped my cheek, thumbing my cheekbone. "Twice isn't really a big risk, but if something happens... I'll take responsibility. Whatever you want to do. When we get home, we'll use condoms."

"Okay." It made me feel warm inside to know Caleb intended for us to be together even after we returned to Minnesota.

"Can I say something and you won't get weird about it?" I asked, threading my fingers through his over his stomach.

Caleb chuckled. "Jacey, anything you want to say, now would be the time to say it, weird or not."

I swallowed, then whispered, "I love you."

CHAPTER 16: LOVE ME, BABY

-Caleb-

When Jocelyn said she loved me, it completely blew away her earlier worry about pregnancy. I wasn't sure I was ready to be a dad, but I did know one thing for certain.

"I love you, too," I said, tilting her lips up to mine for a kiss.

"Not stepbrother/stepsister love, either," Jocelyn clarified, as though she needed to.

I chuckled and kissed her again. "Baby, I'm pretty sure if I felt THAT kind of love for you, we wouldn't be having sex."

"True." Jocelyn licked her lips. I could feel the slightest flick of her tongue against my mouth. "And you don't have to just say it. I don't expect you to say it back just because we might die tomorrow."

"That might have sped up the timeline a bit, but it doesn't make it less true," I said to her, stroking her hair.

"Really?" Jocelyn asked cautiously.

"Really." I did love her. It wasn't something I'd felt for most of the women I'd had. In fact, I was trying to think of anyone I'd have been so willing to die for, who made me so possessive.

Jocelyn was sexy, independent, courageous, and smart. The whole package. And I was a lucky, lucky bastard to have her at last.

Speaking of which...

I slowly slid our joined hands into my pants. "I want to be inside you again. Will you let me?" I taught her how to touch me to get me from my semi to completely erect.

Jocelyn rubbed her thumb over my tip. "I think that would be nice."

I shivered and opened my pants in record time. She still stroked me while I pulled down her pants and panties.

"Show me where you want me, baby," I breathed, nipping her earlobe as her knees spread open beneath me.

Jocelyn guided me right to her entrance. My cum and her juices made it easy to push inside this time, even though she was still deliciously tight.

"Mmm... baby." I rubbed her clit with my thumb, easing in and out of her. My other hand pushed up under her shirt and bra to squeeze a perfect breast.

I was being faster, rougher this time, riding her harder than I had before. Need sang in my blood. She loved me. I loved her. She was mine. MINE.

"Oh GOD, Caleb!" Jocelyn gasped, hanging onto my shoulders for dear life as I lost myself to the passion of the moment.

I knew when she was going to come. I could feel it in the way her body trembled, hear it in the hitch in her breathing. I also knew when I came, I wasn't going to pull out. I should—it was madness to keep risking pregnancy like this—but the possessive side of me that had taken over needed to fill her with my cum.

I quickly molded my mouth to hers when she cried out, shuddering with a powerful orgasm. I thrust three more times, then pushed deep, releasing my entire load into her.

"Caleb..." Jocelyn sighed, accepting my seed without protest.

I slowly nuzzled and sucked her nipples, pushing her bra and shirt out of my way, keeping my cock inside her. I wasn't willing to let this be the end. I was greedy, greedy for her body and her beautiful spirit.

"You're not pulling out," Jocelyn panted after a while. She kept biting her lip to keep from making noise as I worshipped her breasts.

"Nope," I agreed.

Jocelyn's chest heaved, and she cradled my head to her breast. "We're doing it again."

"You bet your sweet ass we are," I said.

I hardened again after a bit as she got hotter and wetter around me from the attention I was giving her breasts. I had to silence little mewls with my lips as I made slow love to her this time, taking her with aching tenderness.

I tasted her tears on my tongue and pulled my mouth from hers to kiss her tears away.

"It's okay, baby," I whispered. "I've got you. I'm here."

Jocelyn wrapped her arms around me and buried her face in my neck, sobbing softly.

I stroked her hair. "Does it feel okay, baby?"

Jocelyn nodded against me.

"Good. It's okay. I know you're scared. I'm scared, too. But we're here and we're together now," I said with a swallow.

Jocelyn's lips brushed my neck, so sweetly I thought I might fucking cry myself.

Instead, I focused on her and her pleasure, listening to her breathing pick up when I thumbed her clit.

When Jocelyn came apart, she whimpered into my shoulder.

Her body squeezed around my cock, and I came with a groan, still buried deep inside her.

I pressed my forehead to hers as we both panted and came down. "Baby, I love you," I whispered to her. "I love you, Jacey."

"I love you, Caleb," Jocelyn responded, making me warm to the center of my bones.

This time, I did pull out and get us back into our clothes, giving Jocelyn tender touches as I did so. Then I wrapped my arms around her and waited for the dawn.

I don't think either of us slept a wink, watching the door, waiting for Fate to come knocking.

Sooner than either of us wanted, the chain jingled heavily, and the door opened. We sat up.

Girard stood in the doorway and leaned against the frame. "Christian did say he heard some interesting sounds last night," he smirked. "You've been fucking your sister."

Jocelyn paled. I looked down at the blanket and, sure enough, there was plenty of evidence of our activities.

"I don't see how that's any of your business," I grunted.

"You kill people. You fuck your sister. You're a sick, sick man," Girard chuckled.

"Have you made a decision?" I asked, ignoring his needling.

Girard shrugged. "Guess you'll have to find out." He stepped out of the doorway, and the man I could only assume was Christian pointed a gun at us.

"Out," Christian said.

I rose, then tugged Jocelyn up. The two of us put our flannel shirts back on, then walked out of the shed, Jocelyn's hand in mine.

Just as we cleared the door, two men jumped up behind us, holding smelly cloths over our faces.

I struggled, losing my grip on Jocelyn.

"Breathe," Girard ordered while Christian kept his gun trained on us.

Jocelyn coughed, gagged, then sagged in the arms of the man who held the cloth.

"Ngh!" I cried in muffled protest, trying to shake my attacker off me and go to her. But two other men came forward and gripped me by the arms.

Girard crossed his arms over his chest. "Breathe."

Contrary to his orders, I held my breath as long as I could. I finally coughed and gasped, burning fumes entering my nose and mouth.

"Keep breathing, son," Girard said.

My vision started to blacken from the outside in.

The last thing I remembered was Christian grinning at Girard. "Least it won't be messy."

I WOKE to the sound of lapping water. Peeling my eyes open, I saw sand, bits of wood, and broken glass. "Jacey?" I mumbled, looking around, trying to orient myself.

Then it all came crashing back, and I sat up straight. "Jacey?!"

Still in the too-big red flannel shirt, pants, and knee-high waders, Jocelyn was lying not five feet from me.

I struggled to my feet, still wearing the steel-toed boots and other clothing I'd "borrowed" from the lumberjacks. We were on a strip of beach, a sandbar, to be exact. There was water on both sides of us, stretching in either direction to swathes of deep forest.

Carefully picking my way around glass and broken boards with rusty nails sticking out, I made it to Jocelyn's side. I shook her gently. "Jacey?"

Jocelyn groaned and was about to roll onto a particularly nasty-looking glass shard before I stopped her.

"There's broken glass everywhere," I explained with my hand firmly on her shoulder. "You need to be careful."

"Broken glass?" Jocelyn echoed. She let me help her to her feet, then looked around.

When she sagged against me, I was sure we'd fallen into some bad trouble. But then she looked up at me with a smile and tears in her eyes. "Caleb, they dropped us at the old fly-in camp!"

"The old fly-in camp?" I said.

"Yes. It's right by our camp. Almost straight across from it. We passed it when we left in the boat," Jocelyn replied excitedly.

My knees turned to jelly, and I had to sit down. As I did so, my pocket crinkled.

I reached in and pulled out a piece of paper and a box of matches.

"What's that?" Jocelyn asked, sitting down next to me. She plucked the paper from my unresisting hands. "'We know what you did. Don't rat us out, or there will be consequences. Burn this letter.'"

I sighed. "Sure, we can burn the letter, but what happens when I have to tell the authorities what happened to Bill? It's not like the logging operation was far away."

Jocelyn stared up at me for a long moment, then she took the matches, struck one on an old board, and set fire to the paper. "We're not going to tell anyone about Bill."

"What?" I said. "Jacey, I killed a man!"

"Nobody needs to know that. Nobody ever needs to know that. I'm sure Girard is taking care of it even as we speak," Jocelyn decided. "He was a bad man. He was going to hurt me. There's no reason you should get in trouble for what happened to him."

"Jacey, I happened to him," I reminded her.

Jocelyn shook her head. "No. We're not going to tell anyone about it. It'll be between you, me..."

"And about twenty-five illegal loggers," I snorted.

Jocelyn took my face in her hands, forcing me to look at her. "We have to come up with some story. Something believable."

"I find the truth is usually pretty believable," I replied.

"Caleb, I forbid you to throw your future away because of that asshole," Jocelyn snapped.

Her beautiful green eyes were shimmering with tears, pleading with me.

I wasn't proof against that. "All right. What do you suggest?"

"We say we managed to walk to the North Lake, and some kind fishermen spotted us, gave us some clothes, and brought us to the fly-in camp. We knew we'd be found from there. That's it. That's all we have to say," Jocelyn said.

"Okay," I responded. "Okay, yeah, that's simple and to the point."

Jocelyn nodded. "Good."

As soon as I'd agreed, I began to hear a buzzing in the background. We both turned to look.

There were two boats coming toward us. One had a man in forest green at the motor. The other, I could tell from his bright blue life-jacket, was being navigated by Hank.

Jocelyn and I both walked to the edge of the water and waved our arms over our heads.

I looked briefly behind us and saw that the note had smoldered completely to ash.

CHAPTER 17: SECRETS

-Jacey-

"... So what you're saying is some kindly fishermen took you to the old fly-in camp and just left you there?" my father said for the thousandth time.

It was a simple lie, but I wasn't used to lying to him. I had to, though, because I didn't want Caleb getting in trouble for what had happened to Bill. I also didn't want the lumberjacks to make good on their threat.

"We told them it was close enough to camp. Then they didn't have to do the pull-through," I explained.

"You should have asked them to bring you all the way to camp," Jeanie added her two cents, her hand on Caleb's shoulder as we sat side-by-side on the picnic table bench in our camp. My father was on my left side. Jeanie was on Caleb's right.

My father nodded his agreement. "That was rather stupid of both of you. On top of stupid."

Caleb scowled and opened his mouth to say something to my father, but I squeezed his knee.

"The conservation officer was just about to call in the Mounties. Do you know that?" my father went on scolding us.

"It was nice of them to give you some clothes," Jeanie said. "But still, it would have been better if they'd brought you back to us."

"Now some perfectly good fishing gear and a boat motor are at the bottom of the lake because you two had to go off in a huff into a storm," my father fumed.

"Gee, glad you were so concerned about us," Caleb cut in sarcastically.

My father stabbed a finger at him. "I'm not done with you yet."

Caleb stood suddenly, Jeanie's hand falling away. "Actually, you are. If you need me, I'll be up on top of the hill." He began stalking off in the direction of the john, then up the hill past it.

My father rose to pursue him, but Jeanie caught his wrist. "Just let him blow off some steam for a little while. I know he knows he did wrong, just like Jacey knows." She turned to me. "We really are just glad you're back in one piece."

If only she knew how iffy that had been. "I'll go after Caleb. Maybe I can talk him down," I offered.

"I suppose, if anything, this trip was a success because you two are actually getting along and not having all this awkward pussyfooting around," my father grumbled.

"We worked everything out while we were lost," I said. "Don't worry. We're okay now."

"Almost worth the loss of a motor." My father stood. "I suppose you can go do Caleb duty while Jeanie and I make dinner. We have a birthday cake here for you. Shame you were lost in the woods on your birthday."

I shrugged. "Thanks for the cake, but Caleb still made the day special."

"Oh?" Jeanie asked. "How so?"

He fucked me senseless under a sky full of shooting stars. "We watched some shooting stars," I smiled.

"That Caleb. He's a good boy," Jeanie said, following my father into the cook tent.

"Don't be too long. Dinner will be ready within half an hour," my father grunted.

I sighed. I really had to impress on Caleb that my father wasn't really that bad a guy, and that he was never going to change.

Now in my tennis shoes and sporting some nice blisters where the boots had rubbed me, I walked up the path to find Caleb.

He was sitting on a large boulder at the top of the hill, drawing with a stick in the scrub grass. When he saw me, Caleb rose and wrapped me in his arms, kissing me hungrily.

"Caleb!" I protested when he shoved a hand up under my shirt and bra.

"Don't say 'no,'" Caleb begged me. "Please."

I knew some of this had to be Caleb screwing me so he could screw over my father, but I also knew he was raw and emotional. Hell, I was raw and emotional.

"Okay," I whispered. "Just not on top of the hill where they could see from the lake."

Caleb nodded and tugged me down the other side of the hill, deeper into the woods. "Take off your clothes," he said, backing me up to a birch tree.

It was mostly smooth with a couple of knots against my back. I stripped off my T-shirt and bra.

Caleb played with my breasts while I shivered and stripped off the rest.

"In a minute, I'm going to lift you onto my dick. When I do, wrap your legs around my waist and hang onto me. Okay?" Caleb murmured.

"Okay." I wondered what was going to take him "a minute" until his lips descended on mine and his fingers pressed up inside me.

"Oh, God, Caleb..." I moaned. He knew just where and how to touch me to get me wet for him.

He opened his pants and rubbed the shaft of his cock against my seam, getting us both slick and ready. Then Caleb lifted me by my thighs and brought me down hard on his cock.

I cried out, but remembered to wrap my legs around his waist, pulling him deeper still. Caleb groaned, and as I gripped his shoulders, he began fucking me against the birch tree. Hard.

It was harder than I was used to from him, but it still felt wonderful. Our bodies coupled desperately, both of us pouring the unresolved emotions of the last few days into our lovemaking.

I could feel Caleb's anger, fear, and anguish in every hard thrust. I knew what he needed, and I gave it to him, every cell of my body tuned to his.

"Baby, you feel so good," Caleb groaned, still keeping up a punishing pace that lit a fire in me.

"You... too..." I panted, my eyes rolling back when his cock rubbed right where I wanted it.

"There?" Caleb asked, hitting the spot again.

"Yes. YES!" I bit my lip against a loud yowl of pleasure as an orgasm rocked me from my core.

Caleb didn't pull out, and I wasn't going to ask him to. He poured every ounce of emotion from our ordeal into one long ejaculation, filling me up with his warm cum.

I held onto him, my arms and legs wrapped around him, stroking my hands up and down his back while he emptied into me.

"Jacey," Caleb sighed as he finished, squeezing my ass. "Fuck, I needed that. Thank you. Thank you so much."

"Don't think you're any less addicting," I teased him.

As he softened again, his cock slipped out of me, and Caleb put me back on the ground. "So, what did your dad have to say when I stomped off on him?"

"Pretty sure he just wanted to yell some more. As long as you didn't take a boat this time, I think he's fine," I said, sliding Caleb's cock back into his pants and zipping him up.

Caleb shook his head. "Your dad is an asshole."

"He's really not. He's just... old school, I guess," I replied. "You have to kind of look between the words. He wasn't actually worried about a motor more than he was worried about us."

"Could have fooled me," Caleb snorted, now helping me back into my panties and pants.

I snapped my bra straps over my shoulders and frowned at him. "Caleb, please try to get along with my father. For my sake."

Caleb knelt to tie my tennis shoe, which had come undone during sex. He impudently poked his tongue in my belly button. "Okay. For you, I'll do it."

"Thank you," I said. "Now—"

"Provided you do something for me," Caleb grinned.

I rolled my eyes. "Caleb, I don't know if your short-term memory is working, but I seem to remember..."

"Let me sleep with you," Caleb interrupted me.

I stared at him. "Pardon?"

Caleb rubbed the back of his neck. "I keep seeing... Bill..." He shook his head. "Forget it. It's a stupid idea." He twitched my T-shirt down to my waist, then started back toward camp.

I caught his wrist. "Caleb, I just have the small cot, and it won't take our weight, but if you bring your sleeping bag, we might be able to zip them together on the ground. We just... can't wake up Dad and Jeanie."

Caleb tugged me to him and wrapped me in a hug, burying his face in my hair. "Thank you, Jacey. Just keep your ears peeled. I'll be there tonight."

"Hey, you two, you're not thinking of running off again, are you?" an anxious call came over the top of the hill.

Caleb and I sprang apart, looking up to see Jeanie at the top of the hill.

"Mom?" Caleb asked. "How long have you been standing there?"

"That was the sweetest hug," Jeanie said, dabbing her eyes. "I'm glad I got to see it. Why does it matter how long I was here?"

"N-No reason," I replied quickly. "Just... well... Caleb was just venting a little about Dad's behavior, and I was hoping you weren't offended."

"Oh. No, I wasn't around for that part. But I do understand. I wish Caleb and Hank didn't butt heads so often," Jeanie sighed.

Caleb scowled at us. "I'm right here. You don't have to talk around me."

Jeanie's laughter was like a tinkling of bells. She really was a sweet woman, and I was glad she didn't walk in on us doing something

Caleb said she thought was "gross." "I'm just here to let you know that dinner is ready."

"Thanks!" Caleb and I said together, a bit sheepishly.

Jeanie started back down the hill.

As soon as she was out of sight, Caleb pulled me against him for a long kiss. "To tide me over," he explained after he let me go.

We walked back to camp, Caleb's hand at my back even though I didn't need the help picking my way over the path. It was a nice, safe, comforting feeling just the same.

My father was still stewing, I could tell. He slapped fresh, fried fish down onto paper plates with angry muttering, causing grease and some fish flakes to fly everywhere.

Jeanie hung on his arm, trying to calm him down.

Caleb tensed the moment he saw my father, but all I had to do was give him one look and he made a concerted effort to relax.

"Sorry for storming off on you like that, Hank," Caleb said, offering the olive branch.

I held my breath and looked at my father.

"What, just now or when you nearly got my daughter killed?" my father spat.

"Dad!" I admonished him before Caleb could say anything. "Caleb followed ME. I went first, remember?"

"Don't remind me," my father muttered. "I know I raised you better than that."

"Hank, please," Jeanie said, leaning her cheek on my father's shoulder.

My father deflated. "There's tartar sauce and lemon slices in the cooler." He picked up his own plate and salad bowl and went to the table.

"That's code for 'let's make peace,'" I whispered to Caleb.

"I think you're going to have to keep translating for me because I heard 'I'm a toddler and I'm going to have a temper tantrum,'" Caleb mumbled back.

"He's probably thinking the same thing about you right now, you know," I pointed out.

That made Caleb laugh. He went into the tent with me, and we both got our fish and our salads and went to the picnic table to sit across from my father and Jeanie.

Since we weren't flinching every time we accidentally brushed each other, it was a nice meal, and even my father had cheered up by the end of it.

Caleb and I took care of the silverware while my dad took the paper dishes and used them as kindling for our evening fire.

It was all so normal, it was hard to believe what had transpired in the last few days.

But the haunted look in Caleb's eyes when he stared off into the distance from time to time made my stomach knot and told me that yes, indeed, everything, good and bad, had really happened.

CHAPTER 18: NOW I LAY ME

-CALEB-

My mom cuddled with Hank while we roasted marshmallows. I envied them that. They laughed together and fed each other sticky s'mores.

Jocelyn and I sat shoulder-to-shoulder on the short, narrow bench on our side of the fire, but I couldn't put my arm around her, and I sure as hell couldn't go licking marshmallow off her fingers like Hank was doing to my mother.

It was our first taste, I guess, of what life was going to be like outside the little bubble we'd created when we'd been lost.

"Want half my Hershey bar?" I asked Jocelyn, trying to distract from our parents acting like kids.

"Sure." Jocelyn herself looked a bit wistful.

I swore to myself, the first chance I got, I was renting us a cabin in the middle of nowhere where we could tease each other, and laugh, and touch, and fuck all we wanted without anyone around to judge us.

I set a cool piece of chocolate on half a graham cracker for her, holding the other half of the graham cracker above it so Jocelyn could slide her toasted marshmallow inside. The chocolate began to melt on my thumb, and I licked it off suggestively while I handed her the finished s'more.

Jocelyn blushed. "Stop it," she breathed, though we both knew her father and my mother were too wrapped up in each other to notice.

I just grinned.

"Say, Caleb, your marshmallow's going to burn to a crisp," Hank suddenly said.

I looked down at the stick I was absently holding over the fire and, sure enough, my marshmallow was mostly ash.

"Guess it's kindling now," Hank chuckled. He passed his stick to me. "I think Jeanie and I are finished. You go ahead and eat that one. It's a nice golden brown."

I didn't know if it was my mother's influence, or Jocelyn's, or just another side of Hank's nature, but he was trying to warm up to me at least. "Thanks," I replied.

Hank smiled and tugged my mother up off their bench. "Make sure to put out the fire before you head to bed."

There was a bucket of sand sitting next to the fire for just that purpose. "I will. Thanks, Hank."

"You're welcome, son," Hank said. He clapped me on the shoulder as he and my mother walked past us, giggling like two teenagers as they went to the air mattress inside their tent.

Hank winked at me before he zipped the tent flap shut.

It might have needled me before, but I was fucking his daughter, so... I guessed we were even.

Jocelyn leaned her head on my shoulder. "Back to reality."

"Reality's changed a bit, though, hasn't it?" I said softly, kissing her hair.

"True." Jocelyn tipped her head up and kissed me.

I kissed her back, thoroughly, until she was panting and clinging to me.

I'd even forgotten that Hank and my mother were twenty feet away, doing God only knew what, until I heard Hank snoring.

I smiled and took Jocelyn's hand, kissing the palm. "Jacey," I murmured, "let's go to bed."

"Okay." Jocelyn gave me a last peck on the lips then went to dump sand on the embers of the fire.

I grabbed her ass while she was bent over with the bucket, and Jocelyn swatted my hand. My grin was absolutely unrepentant in the flashlight glow as she turned hers on and shined it in my face.

"We have to be quiet," she reminded me. "Get your sleeping bag."

I turned on my flashlight and gave her an impulsive kiss. "Yes, ma'am."

Jocelyn shook her head and muttered something about me being incorrigible before padding off to her tent.

I waited a few beats then went to my own tent, grabbing my sleeping bag off my cot and zipping the door flap closed behind me.

"Knock knock," I whispered at Jocelyn's tent.

She pushed her tent flap open, letting me inside.

In the light of our flashlights, I could see that Jocelyn had pushed a stack of clothes, books, and toiletries under her cot to make room for our sleeping bags.

I zipped the tent flap closed behind me then went about figuring out how to zip our sleeping bags together.

As we both had weather-appropriate sleeping bags which tapered at the foot, it was a bit of a feat, but I managed it at last. I stripped down to my boxers and snuggled down into the doubled-up sleeping bags.

Jocelyn stripped to panties and a T-shirt and followed me inside. I zipped us in, and we both laid our heads on Jocelyn's pillow, cocooned together without an inch of space between our bodies.

"Now we're going to go to sleep. SLEEP," Jocelyn instructed me in a no-nonsense tone.

I had to say, my dick was disappointed by her edict, but we both needed the rest. I put an arm around Jocelyn and spread my hand under her shirt, over her bare back, but did not go any further.

Jocelyn closed her eyes, and we turned off our flashlights. I breathed her in, letting her scent and feel comfort me. In truth, I was afraid to go to sleep. Every time I closed my eyes, I could see Bill's bashed-in skull.

I must have fallen asleep, though, because I woke with a start with Jocelyn's hand over my mouth.

"Caleb," she whispered, kissing my temple. "Caleb, it's me, it's okay. It's okay. I'm here."

I was covered in cold sweat, even though we were inside the sleeping bags, pressed together. I couldn't even remember what I'd been dreaming, but it must not have been anything good, because Jocelyn was muffling, if I had to guess by the rawness in my throat, a scream.

"What's going on?" Hank asked, his feet pounding the ground to our tents. "Jacey? Did you scream?"

"I..." Jocelyn replied loudly, keeping her hand over my mouth. "I... thought there was a spider in my sleeping bag.

Hank groaned outside her tent. "Jacey, it's three o'clock in the morning."

"I know. I'm sorry. I was asleep and I felt something crawling," Jocelyn said.

"Oh dear. That sounds awful," my mother's voice joined in.

"It was," Jocelyn responded. "It was awful. But then it turned out it was just the tag on the sleeping bag, so everything's fine. Sorry I woke everyone up."

Hank chuckled. "Everyone but Caleb. Boy sleeps like a rock."

"Right," Jocelyn said. "Well, that's good."

"Let's try to keep screaming to a minimum, okay?" Hank's voice was kind and filled with humor.

"Absolutely. Sorry, Dad. Jeanie," Jocelyn replied contritely.

Our parents walked off, and I could hear their tent flap zip open.

Jocelyn snuggled into me and stroked my hair, comforting me.

I buried my face in her neck, taking deep breaths.

"Maybe we should just try to stay awake," Jocelyn suggested.

"Okay. That sounds like a plan," I said, unzipping the sleeping bags to get a little air on my skin.

Jocelyn laid her cheek on my shoulder and stroked my chest, belly, and sides as the sweat began to evaporate off my skin.

I closed my eyes and let her touch chase away my demons. At least for a little while.

Then Jocelyn's hand slid under the waistband of my boxers and circled my cock.

I grunted softly, putting my hand over hers as she stroked my shaft gently.

"Jacey," I whispered into her hair when she ran her thumb over my tip. My dick was screaming for release, but I didn't want to cum in her hand.

I rolled us so she was underneath me. I could hear Jocelyn's surprise in the sharp intake of her breath.

Fusing my lips to hers, I began tugging down her panties.

Jocelyn whimpered against my lips when I cupped her mound and began getting her wet with my fingers.

"I want to cum inside, baby. Will you let me?" I murmured in her ear.

I felt Jocelyn nod against my cheek.

When her juices were dripping over my hand, I replaced my fingers with my straining cock, pushing in sharply to the hilt. I swallowed Jocelyn's cry of surprise.

"I'm so close, baby. This is gonna be hard and fast, but I'll make you come first," I promised, beginning a punishing pace. I knew how she liked it. I knew where she liked it. And I hit the spot with every thrust.

Jocelyn clung to my shoulders, making little sounds of pleasure against my lips. Then I had to stifle a shriek from her with my palm as her body found sweet release.

I bit the inside of my cheek against a groan as I jetted into her, finding my own release.

We were going to have to invest in condoms when we got home. Lots, and lots, and lots of condoms. And maybe an EPT, given the number of times I'd cum in her and the number of times I was going to cum in her by the time we left.

"Baby, I need to go back to my tent," I sighed after we came down and I was able to withdraw my softening cock from her body. "I don't want to, but I think Hank and Mom might have something to say if they see me sneaking out of your tent after they wake up in the morning."

Jocelyn combed her fingers through my hair and caressed my cheek. "Are you going to be okay?"

"Yeah. I'll read a book," I replied. I kissed her nose. "I love you, Jacey."

"I love you, Caleb." Jocelyn's lips sought mine, but I had to break away after a few minutes with a laugh.

"Jacey, we're going to end up doing it well past breakfast if we keep kissing like THAT," I warned her.

Jocelyn nuzzled my neck, but gave in, starting to separate our sleeping bags. "I wish we could."

"Me, too," I admitted. "Maybe we can stay back tomorrow. Hank was talking about trying to crowd all of us in the one boat, but maybe he and Mom just want to have some alone time, too."

"This is already so complicated," Jocelyn groaned. "I don't even know how we'll do this when we get home."

"Simple. I'll visit you all the time on campus and practically move into your dorm," I teased.

Jocelyn swatted my shoulder. "I'm being serious."

"Me, too," I grinned. Then I sobered and hugged Jocelyn to me. "We're going to work it out. I promise."

"Okay," Jocelyn said. "As long as I have your solemn word on that."

"You do. On my honor," I replied. "We're going to figure out how to be together."

Jocelyn squeezed my hand in acknowledgement. "Okay, you. You need to go back to your tent." She gave me a playful smack on the ass.

I inwardly vowed to return the favor. I kissed her one last time, then snuck out of her tent with my sleeping bag over my shoulder.

Somehow, we were going to work this out.

CHAPTER 19: STOLEN MOMENTS

-Jacey-

It didn't take much convincing for my father and Jeanie to go out fishing alone. I was pretty sure our ordeal had put a crimp in their romantic getaway plans, so when Caleb and I suggested we were too tired to go out fishing, my father and Jeanie nearly pranced down to the shoreline to launch themselves away from us.

Any other time, I might have been angry about it. I mean, after being checked out by a couple of Canadian medics after our disappearance and declared perfectly fit, my father and Jeanie hadn't worried one bit about it. But their being all wrapped up in each other meant Caleb and I had less trouble concealing our own activities.

Today's activities started with Caleb bending me over the picnic table and screwing me senseless. The angle meant he went deeper than he'd been in me before, his cock touching places I hadn't known existed.

I was learning a lot about Caleb's preferences, and he was learning my body better than I knew it myself. He seemed to consider it the best game ever to find new places to touch and explore that would make me gasp.

Caleb, I knew, preferred to cum inside me. No matter what kind of fooling around we started with, he always wanted to end buried deep in my vagina.

We had a lot of time to discover these things about each other as I knew day fishing could last past 2:00 in the afternoon.

I laid, exhausted after two hours, with my head in Caleb's lap, stretched out on the picnic bench.

Caleb stroked my hair while playing a game of solitaire on the table.

"Caleb?" I asked after a while. "Are you going to want to wear a condom when we get home?"

Caleb's fingers stilled, and he looked down at me. "I don't know if any man wants to wear a condom as opposed to going bareback, but it's the responsible thing to do. Even if you go on birth control, we might have to use condoms for a little bit before it kicks in, depending on what you get."

"I was thinking about an IUD," I said. "Then we won't have to worry about it."

"All right. Whatever you choose. I'm a big boy. I can wear a condom," Caleb chuckled.

I blushed. "I like feeling you cum in me."

Caleb's eyebrows raised, and he looked very pleased with himself. "Glad I can be of service."

I rolled my eyes and swatted his ass, which was the closest thing I could reach. "You don't have to be so smug."

"Oh, I think I do," Caleb replied. "I'm turning you into my own little sex maniac."

"Ugh, YOU'RE the sex maniac! I don't think they were out of sight of camp before you started drilling me over the picnic table!" I said defensively.

Caleb shrugged. "Didn't want to wait. I couldn't. Fuck, Jacey, you make me want to do things..."

I giggled. "Yeah, I know you want to do things. Lots of things. I want to, too, but holy Christ, Caleb, you've got the stamina of a... of a... something with lots of stamina."

"What can I say? I'm inspired." Caleb booped my nose.

"You're going to make me sore," I pouted.

Caleb reached down and fondled my breast through my shirt. "You're going to love it."

That made me blush because he wasn't wrong.

Caleb started rubbing my nipple in slow circles, and I groaned, feeling his dick stiffening under my cheek. "Really?"

"Remember, I have the stamina of something with lots of stamina," Caleb teased.

I sat up, then stood and shimmied my pants and panties down a little, bending over the table.

"Take them all the way off. I want you to ride me," Caleb said, opening his pants and taking out his positively massive dick. He was already leaking precum, and I felt desire deep in my loins.

I kicked my pants and panties off over my shoes and let Caleb take my hand, steadying me while he laid down on the bench and I swung a leg over and straddled him.

"Stand up a little and... there you go. Yeah, baby, line it up with your hole and just sit down slowly..." Caleb hissed as I slid down his shaft.

My eyelids fluttered. "Caleb, it's... it's going too deep..."

"You can do it, baby. Take it all in." Caleb massaged my bare hips, helping me ease down onto him until I was sitting on his hips with his cock all the way inside me, deeper than I'd thought was possible. "Just sit still a minute. Then rock a little on my dick and see how it feels."

I took several deep breaths as my body adjusted to him. After a few minutes, I started rocking, and shivered at the feel.

"Pull your shirt and bra up, baby. I want to see those big tits bounce," Caleb groaned, his hands still on my hips, guiding my movements as I started to ride him.

With a soft laugh, I did him one better and pulled my shirt and bra off. I touched the ground with the balls of my feet, using that and my hands on his chest to gain traction as I moved on him.

Caleb watched my breasts while I started letting out little sounds of need. As though he knew exactly what I needed, Caleb gripped my hips and started encouraging me to ride him harder, faster, and at a slightly different angle.

My tits swung in his face, and Caleb licked and sucked on my nipples. Soon the woods were filled with the sound of the wet slapping of our bodies coming together and both our grunts and sighs of desire.

"Come for me, baby. Let me feel that sweet hole of yours squeezing my cock," Caleb panted.

I shivered at his words, just enough to push me over the edge. I pressed my palms over Caleb's nipples and arched my back like a cat, crying out as an orgasm rushed through me.

Caleb came then as well, ejaculating into me with a groan.

"Did you like that, baby?" he asked me, gripping my ass so he was pushed in as deep as he could get. "Do you like my hot cum?"

"Mhm," I whimpered, surprised at how turned on I felt when he talked that way.

"Yeah, I know you do." Caleb kissed me then pulled me down on top of him so I was resting on his chest.

I snuggled into him, well aware that he still had a semi inside me, knowing he'd want to take care of that in a few minutes. I decided all the sexy talk turned him on, too.

"When we get home," Caleb said, twisting my braid around his fist. "I'm going to undo your hair so it falls all around while we're having sex. It's so soft."

"Maybe I'll just have to wear my hair down more often. When we get home. It's not really practical here," I laughed.

Caleb gave my hair a light tug so my face tilted up, then devoured my mouth.

I could barely breathe, and I didn't care. All I wanted was more. Maybe he was making me into a sex maniac.

"You're so perfect," Caleb sighed after we made out for several minutes.

"You say that a lot," I smiled, nuzzling his stubbly cheek.

"Doesn't make it any less true. I am a lucky sonofabitch. When I'm a doctor, I'm gonna take good care of you," Caleb mused.

I framed his face with my hands and gave him a soft peck on the lips. "You already take good care of me."

Caleb chuckled and stroked my back absently. "I'm glad you think so. But seriously, I'm going to get my medical degree, and then we'll be able to build a life together. Not sneaking around."

I felt warm all over and hugged Caleb, tucking my head under his chin. "I like that you think about a future with me in it."

"Don't you?" Caleb asked, his hand stilling on my back.

"Ever since I was fifteen. I just... um... never thought... it'd become a real possibility, you know?" I said.

"Well, believe it. You're stuck with me now," Caleb chuckled.

I gave a happy little sigh. "Good."

Caleb's cock twitched and swelled inside me, and it was my turn to chuckle. "I think somebody's feeling a little neglected," I teased.

"Mmm, so neglected. I mean, I never get any," Caleb deadpanned.

I burst out laughing. "Right. Never."

"Sit up, baby. I'm gonna do you in my lap," Caleb said.

I sat up, and so did Caleb, fully erect now.

I kissed Caleb softly while he gripped my hips and moved me up and down on his cock. Fast. Desperate.

"Ah... ah... ah..." I made little yips each time he plunged inside me.

"Mmm, yeah, baby. Do you like my big dick?" Caleb asked, nibbling my collarbone.

"Yes..." I moaned.

"Yes what?" Caleb prompted.

"Yes, I like your big dick," I panted.

Caleb grinned against my skin and slammed my hips against his, his cock like a piston inside me. "You feel so good, baby. Hot, wet, tight. How do I feel?"

"B-Big." My body was starting to tremble, and I knew my orgasm wasn't far off. "H-Hard. Oh God, I feel so FULL..."

"You want me to fill you up, don't you," Caleb grunted. "Tell me what your sweet hole wants."

"I want you to push all the way in," I moaned. "And I want you to fill me up with your cum."

Caleb groaned at my words and thumbed my clit while he bounced me on his cock until I came hard around him.

Then Caleb gripped my hips and pushed as deep as he could, and filled me up with his hot cum again. He groaned as he kept spurting, caught in the throes of a powerful orgasm.

I fluttered kisses over his face while he finished with one last twitch of his cock. I was pretty sure he was giving me everything he had, leaving nothing left in his balls.

Caleb held me there in his lap, and I leaned my cheek on his shoulder. "Oh... fuck... baby that was so good."

"Mhm," I agreed with a yawn.

Caleb chuckled. "Aw, here's me getting my baby all tired out." He very gently pulled me off his softening dick. "Why don't you get dressed and take another nap with your head in my lap."

That sounded like a fantastic idea, and I smiled at him. "Maybe when I wake up, we can play cards. CARDS. You know, spend time together with you NOT cock deep in me."

Caleb gave a fake pout, and I burst into a fit of giggles.

"No, really, I like that idea, too," Caleb said.

CHAPTER 20: THE LONG ROAD HOME

―

-Jacey-

Because the canoe was a complete loss, it took two trips to get all our gear back to the landing. My father insisted on running both, dropping Jeanie and me off at the landing and hauling the rest with Caleb.

I wasn't sure what they talked about, but Caleb did not return to the landing looking particularly happy.

"I'm so glad you two got back to us safe," Jeanie said for the thousandth time, hugging us both under each arm.

"And that you finally learned how to be a good brother and sister," my father added.

"Stepbrother," Caleb corrected him.

My father shrugged. "Same difference."

"Big difference," Caleb gritted out.

"Oh no. You two aren't going to fight again, are you?" Jeanie asked, her eyes welling with tears.

I was pretty sure Caleb was making the distinction in deference to the fact I'd sucked his cock not six hours ago. I smiled and took Jeanie's hand. "We're not going to fight."

"And you're not going to fight with Hank?" Jeanie said desperately to her son.

I could almost hear Caleb counting backward from twenty in his mind. "No," he replied, "I won't fight with Hank."

"Oh, you're such a love," Jeanie smiled, hugging her son again.

"Oi, if you're done being all lovey-dovey over there, this Suburban isn't going to load itself," my father said.

Caleb got a look on his face that I'd learned to interpret as dangerous. Well, not dangerous exactly. More like rebellious. And that rebelliousness usually manifested itself... inside me.

Though we had sex out of love and commitment to each other, I knew there was a tiny part of Caleb that was comforted by the fact he was screwing Hank's daughter right under his nose.

"I think I'll hit the head," Caleb stated then, giving me a significant look. "Jacey, you need to go before we leave?"

Code: Jacey, I think you need to give me head before we leave.

I frowned at Caleb and shook my head sharply. "No, I'm good."

"Hurry up," my father grunted. "You two always holding us up, ruining the trip..."

Anger flashed in my gut.

"You know what? It's a long time until the first gas station. I think I'll go, too," I said.

"Ugh. That'll take even longer. Women and their..." my father muttered under his breath.

I didn't catch the rest because I was following Caleb into the woods.

Caleb started undoing his pants before we were even out of sight of the landing. Once we were completely away from prying eyes, he pulled out his dick.

I knelt on the ground without being asked and took him in my mouth.

Caleb wrapped my braid around his hand and used it to anchor me to him. But, per our previous agreement, he did not try to shove himself down my throat and choke me.

I sucked Caleb until he was hard and was prepared to keep going, but he pulled me off his cock just as I was starting to swallow the first drops of his precum.

"Get on all fours," Caleb said in a strained voice.

With a nod, I did so. Caleb knelt behind me and reached around to unzip my jeans, before pulling both my jeans and panties down to my knees. Then he shoved one hand up under my shirt and bra to massage my breast while pushing two fingers inside me.

He didn't need to bother. I was wet for him. I was always wet for him. But Caleb was a considerate lover, and I appreciated that.

I felt my juices dripping down the insides of my thighs before Caleb finally withdrew his fingers and slid his dick in where they had been. I moaned as he grabbed my hips and pulled me back sharply, forcing me to take every glorious inch of him in one hard thrust.

"You like that, baby?" Caleb whispered, his balls slapping against me as he began fucking me hard and fast.

"Uh-huh," I managed, feeling his dick go deep with every thrust.

Caleb kept up the pace, gripping my hips and slamming me back onto him over and over. He moved his thumb in to rub my clit. "Baby, are you close?"

"Ah... ah... yes..." I gasped. Two more thrusts sent me right over the edge, and I came around Caleb's cock.

With a groan, Caleb filled me up with his cum. I felt it trickle out of me along with my juices when he pulled out.

Caleb quickly pulled some Kleenex out of his pocket and mopped me up while I sank down onto my elbows, panting.

"You're my good girl," Caleb murmured, kissing my ass cheek before tugging my panties back up. "My sweet baby."

"I am. I'm your baby," I said tiredly, wobbling to my feet with Caleb's help. He pulled up my jeans and zipped them, then got my breast back into my bra and pulled down my shirt.

I tucked his dick away after giving it a loving little kiss, and zipped up Caleb's jeans. I looked up at Caleb and blushed, not sure how to formulate what I wanted to say next. What I needed to say.

Caleb caressed my cheek while I dusted my hands over my knees to clear off pine needles and other debris. "What's the matter?"

I bit my lip. "I'm just not... sure... it's such a good idea... to revenge fuck... every time my dad pisses us off."

"Why? You afraid we'll never stop fucking?" Caleb chuckled. He sobered when he saw the look on my face. "You don't think I'm with you just to give your dad the finger behind his back, do you?"

"N-No..." I said evasively.

"Aw, baby, I'm sorry. I'm being a dick if that's what you're starting to think." Caleb wrapped his arms around me and pulled me against his chest. "That's not why I'm with you at all."

I played with the hem of his shirt. "I know. I just..."

Caleb tilted my head up and kissed me soundly on the mouth. "I love you, Jacey. That's why we make love. And we'll stop fucking just because your dad pisses me off now and then. You're right. It's not a good precedent to set in our relationship."

"Thanks, Caleb," I replied with a smile.

Caleb kissed me again, then we broke apart, and he swatted me playfully on the ass. "Better be getting back. I'll let you go first. Show him girls don't always take the longest."

I giggled. "He's still going to complain."

"Let him. We'll be on the road soon enough, whether he complains or not," Caleb said.

"You going to play sudoku again?" I asked, giving my ass a little wiggle as I started back.

"Nah. No need to distract myself this time. I've got what I want," Caleb grinned.

It warmed me inside to know he'd been trying to distract himself from me just as much as I'd been trying to distract myself from him. And that we didn't have to do that anymore.

Sure enough, when I walked out of the woods and into the scrub brush, my father was pacing next to the packed Suburban.

"Oh good, you're back," he grunted. "Where's Caleb? Shouldn't take a man longer than it takes a woman."

I shrugged innocently. "I'm not sure, Dad. We didn't cross paths."

"Pretty soon I'm sending you right back out there to find him," my father grumbled.

"What if he's... you know..." Jeanie said, putting a hand on my father's arm. "It wouldn't be appropriate for Jacey to see her brother that way."

"Stepbrother," I corrected without thinking.

"Oh dear. You two ARE fighting again," Jeanie sighed unhappily.

"We're not fighting," I said quickly. "It's just..."

"Just what?" my father asked.

"I... it... we..." I stuttered.

Luckily, Caleb made his appearance right at that moment. "Why's everybody frowning?"

"Are you and your sister fighting?" Jeanie's voice quavered.

"No," Caleb said. "But she's my stepsister."

"See? There you go again! What's the difference?" my father demanded.

"The difference is we're not blood related," Caleb explained.

"So? She's your sister. You're her brother. If you weren't acting like it, I'd smack you both upside the head," my father complained. "We're all a family now, and we're going to act like one. Maybe we should all have gotten lost in the woods."

"I don't recommend it," Caleb muttered.

My father glowered at him and opened his mouth to say something, but Jeanie put her hand on his arm again. "Let's just get in the truck and start for home," she suggested.

Grumbling under his breath, my father nodded and headed for the driver's seat.

Caleb and I squeezed into the back next to some gear while Jeanie took the passenger seat.

"You really should let Caleb sit up here because of the leg room," Jeanie said to my father, even as she was buckling her seatbelt.

"The boy can suffer. 'Stepsister' 'stepbrother,' ugh. It's like they're trying to piss me off," my father grumped, starting the Suburban.

Caleb pulled a scratchy flannel blanket out of the back of the Suburban and draped it over us as the Suburban slowly began to warm up. We bumped along the gravel road, holding hands under the blanket while my father openly held Jeanie's hand up front.

When we had to stop for a logging truck, Caleb's grip tightened, both of us remembering the tense day we'd had with the illegal loggers.

"Damn those things kick up a lot of dust," my father groused as we pulled back onto the gravel road, enveloped in a dirt cloud.

I didn't know how my father saw anything at all, and wondered if he actually COULD see anything the way we bumped and bobbed into every deep pothole on the road.

The way Caleb's breathing began to wheeze, I realized he was feeling claustrophobic. I squeezed his hand and stroked his thigh with my thumb.

It calmed him a bit. Caleb squeezed his eyes shut, pretending to sleep.

"Asleep already? Wonder what has the boy so tuckered out," my father mused.

"Probably carrying all the gear back and forth," Jeanie said, smiling back at us. "You should take a nap, too, Jacey. We were up very early this morning."

"True," I agreed. I closed my eyes, but, like Caleb, only pretended to sleep.

"When do you think we should tell them?" Jeanie asked after a while.

My father chuckled. "Would have been on Jacey's birthday, but that got screwed up."

"I still don't know how they'll take it," Jeanie said. "I'm still worried it wasn't the best idea. I'm going to need help, and your work schedule—"

"Jacey'll come home on the weekends," my father replied dismissively. "And seems Caleb's going to be staying with us for at least a year before he gets it together and goes on with his medical degree."

"True." Jeanie was silent a while, then continued. "Do you really think they won't mind?"

"Of course they won't mind. They'll be thrilled to have a little brother or sister to take care of," my father assured her.

Caleb's grip on my hand tightened so much it hurt. I'd dug my other hand into my thigh, anger sparking through me. My father and Jeanie were having a baby, and expecting US to take care of it?!

"I don't want to ruin Jacey's college experience—" Jeanie began.

"Then don't," Caleb said suddenly, his eyes flying open. His cheeks were flushed with rage, and I squeezed his hand several times, but it didn't seem to help. "Grow up, Mom. It's your baby. You take care of it."

Jeanie hitched a sob. "You're not happy about the baby?"

"About being a live-in babysitter while I'm trying to work, and Jacey's having her first year of college? Not so much, no," Caleb snapped. "And stop twisting this around. You want me to see Jacey as my sister? Fine. But that makes you her mother. And no real mother would sacrifice the happiness of one child for another."

Jeanie burst into tears, and my father looked positively murderous as he glared at Caleb in the rearview mirror, his eyes darting occasionally to me in disappointment, even though I hadn't said a thing.

"Don't make me come back there," my father growled.

"Oh, bring it, you old misogynistic sonofabitch," Caleb shot back.

The Suburban fishtailed as my father stomped down on the brakes. "That's it. Out. You're walking."

Caleb undid his seatbelt. "Fine by me." He started crawling over me.

I undid my own seatbelt and followed him.

"Just where the fuck do you think you're going?!" my father snarled at me.

"Walking. If Caleb's walking, I'm walking. And thanks so much. This has been the best birthday EVER," I said sarcastically, hopping out of the Suburban after Caleb and slamming the door behind me.

I wasn't sure if he'd actually do it or not, but after about five minutes of muffled voices in the Suburban, my father stepped on the gas and left us in the dust.

CHAPTER 21: MADE FOR WALKING

-Caleb-

As the dust kicked up around us, I reached for Jocelyn's hand and squeezed it.

"I wonder how far he'll make us walk," Jocelyn said, but her tone indicated she didn't really care.

"At least I have shoes this time," I pointed out with a grin.

Jocelyn giggled then coughed on the dust.

I fanned the air with my free hand, but it didn't seem to help. "We'll have to give him some lead time, otherwise we're going to be walking in a dust cloud all the way."

"Good point," Jocelyn rasped.

I decided we didn't need to wait in the cloud while the dust settled and pulled Jocelyn into the woods to let her cough it out. I wished I'd had the presence of mind to grab a couple of water bottles before jumping out of the Suburban.

"You don't really see me as your sister, do you?" Jocelyn asked after she finished coughing.

I snorted. "Not likely. I see you as my lover. My girlfriend. But definitely not my sister. I was just trying to make a point."

Jocelyn gave me the most beautiful smile, and my heart melted. "Am I your girlfriend?"

"Yep. And I'm your boyfriend. And that's what we are," I said firmly.

"Good." Jocelyn wrapped her arms around my waist and hugged me, pressing her cheek against my shoulder.

I wrapped my arms around her, too. "I'm not going to let them make us live-in babysitters. And I can't believe they'd planned on dropping that bomb on your eighteenth birthday. I mean, that's a big day for you, something to be celebrated. Not something to be overshadowed by some pregnancy announcement."

"I thought my birthday was perfect the way it was," Jocelyn replied softly.

Remembering the sweet way she'd arched beneath me while she gave me her virginity, every precious sound, just made a sense of awe wash over me. I'd treasure that night forever. "I'm glad. I'm still just so... honored you chose me."

Jocelyn leaned up and kissed me. "Who else would I have chosen?"

"I don't know, but the idea of it makes me want to punch him," I chuckled.

"Now we're punching imaginary lovers?" Jocelyn laughed.

"Guess so." I kissed her again on the lips then sucked the spot I'd made on her neck.

"Caleb, we can't!" Jocelyn gasped.

I groaned. "Why not?"

"What if Dad circles back?" Jocelyn pointed out. "Plus there are any number of fishermen and loggers on the road today."

"Like our friends?" I asked.

Jocelyn shivered. "Don't remind me. I really thought they were going to kill us."

"Yeah," I said, "me, too."

Of course, those thoughts brought back Bill, and I remembered, again, how his skull looked all crushed in. It made me want to be sick.

Jocelyn touched my cheek, bringing me out of my horror. "Hey. Don't go there. That was not your fault. He was going to hurt me,

Caleb. Hurt me very badly and probably kill me after. I... I know it's a horrible memory for you but... but... I'm so grateful."

I gave her a wan smile and ran a hand over her hair. "I'm glad he didn't hurt you. I'm... glad I was there."

Jocelyn hugged me tightly.

I looked out to the road and saw the dust had died down. "Okay, I think we can start walking."

Jocelyn nodded and took my hand again. We walked along the side of the road, ready to jump off again if a logger or a fisherman passed.

It was a cool day, which was also a good thing. I sweated just the same, and Jocelyn wiped her sleeve over her brow a few times.

We must have walked at least five miles before we saw the Suburban and boat trailer pulled off to the side of the road.

I looked at Jocelyn. She looked at me. Then, we both just kept walking.

A door slammed and Hank came running up to us. "Don't be stupid. Get in the truck."

"It's a nice day today, isn't it, Jacey? Good day for a nice, long walk to a bus station," I mused.

"I was thinking the same thing," Jocelyn said.

Hank grabbed my shoulder, but I slapped his hand away. "If you want to be helpful, toss us a couple of waters and then fuck off," I growled.

"Boy, you don't get to talk to me that way!" Hank barked, but I ignored him.

Jocelyn tugged on my hand, and we kept walking forward.

"Do you have your passport with you?" Jocelyn whispered to me when Hank finally gave up and got into the Suburban, following us at a crawl.

"Yes. And my wallet. You?" I said.

"Just my passport. But I'll pay you back if you get me a bus ticket," Jocelyn replied quickly.

I chuckled and barely restrained myself from slipping my arm around her waist. "Don't even think about it. We'll call it my birthday present to you."

"But you already gave me such a nice birthday present," Jocelyn said.

Remembering being inside her tight, hot, wet body as the sky filled with shooting stars made my balls tighten. I swallowed and tried to think un-sexy thoughts. "I thought it was a nice present, too, but that was sort of a mutual present. You know, something we both enjoyed."

"Well, so would a bus ride with you," Jocelyn pointed out.

"I think anything involving the two of us together would be a mutual gift," I said.

Jocelyn smiled at me, and we continued walking easily down the road with Hank rolling along in our wake.

"Caleb, Jacey, please get in the truck. Hank is sorry," my mother called out the other window after a while. "We both are. Please, can we talk about this?"

I draped my arm companionably around Jocelyn's shoulders as a way of protecting her from any guilt my mother might be stirring up at that moment. "Nope."

"Jacey, get your ASS in this truck!" Hank shouted. "Unless you want me to revoke your college tuition!"

Ah, there it was. The same carrot he was dangling for me. My jaw worked, and a feeling of bitterness coiled in my stomach like a snake ready to strike. "You know, Hank..."

Jocelyn put a hand on my chest, and I stopped walking. She'd turned very pale. "Let's just get in the Suburban."

I lowered my voice. "You sure?"

"Yes," Jocelyn said. "I can't get financial aid because of how much money Dad makes, and he'll never co-sign for a student loan so..."

She was in the same boat I was. Damn Hank Collins anyway. "Okay. Okay, baby."

I climbed in the Suburban ahead of her so she wasn't the one riding hump and pulled her in next to me. We both buckled up in silence.

Hank was still fuming. As soon as the door was closed and our seatbelts clicked, he stomped on the gas, and we went careening and bumping down the road.

I prayed no logging trucks came from either direction, because the way Hank was driving, there would be zero time to react.

As though we were psychically connected, my mother let out a gasp. "Hank, please, not so fast! Think of the baby!"

Hank slowed down immediately. "Sorry, darling."

Jocelyn and I had probably worn the soles of our tennis shoes straight through on that gravel road, but God forbid something happen to my mother and her precious cargo. If I didn't also love my mother, I'd have been enraged. As it was, I was angry on Jocelyn's behalf.

She must have sensed I was about to let loose on Hank because Jocelyn dug her nails into my knee. I sighed and patted her hand gently.

"I just don't see why you don't want to help with the baby," my mother said after a while.

"I just don't see why you're having a baby if you can't take care of it yourself," I grunted back.

"Family takes care of family," Hank intoned from the driver's seat as though he were Moses coming down the mountain with the Ten Commandments.

I squeezed my eyes shut and counted backward from fifty while Jocelyn's nails dug into my knee again. "Hank, WE'RE family, too. How is it taking care of us to add something new and time-consuming to our plates when we're already doing the school thing?"

"You're not doing 'the school thing,'" Hank said.

"I'm working. I'm padding my resume so I look better to universities AFTER the next stretch," I explained patiently. "I'm going to be busy. Very busy."

Hank glanced at me in the rearview mirror. "Maybe you should start paying rent. A thousand bucks a month sounds good."

"Hank!" my mother cut in, scandalized. "Of course he shouldn't pay rent!"

"If I'm paying that kind of rent, I'm getting my own apartment," I seethed, ignoring the pricks of Jocelyn's fingernails. "And I won't be coming back to take care of any baby. In fact, I might do that anyway."

Hank's face went almost purple. "Why you ungrateful..."

"Why don't you pull over and let us walk again? Teach us a real lesson," I mocked him.

"Hank, just let it go," my mother pleaded. "I guess we were wrong to think they would help."

"Both of you are ungrateful bastards," Hank snarled. "I expected this kind of crap from you, Caleb, but Jacey? I am very surprised and disappointed."

Jocelyn hung her head. "I suppose I could come home on weeke—"

"The hell you will," I interrupted her. "You need to enjoy college. Next thing you know, they'll have you driving back and forth from college to take care of the kid so they can act like a couple of honeymooners instead of parents. If you need help, hire somebody. Jesus."

Hank was so red with rage he looked as though he'd explode. "I'm dropping you two at the bus station. You can find your own way home. I won't spend another minute longer than I have to with you."

"Fine by me," I snapped. "The feeling's mutual."

Jocelyn leaned her head against the seat back and squeezed her eyes closed.

"Is that true, Jacey? Is the feeling mutual?" Hank asked.

"I'll go with Caleb. I need time to think," Jacey said softly.

"Think about what? We're family. We take care of each other," Hank scoffed. "You're going to have a little brother or sister..."

"Dad, I don't want to talk about it. Because if we talk about it now, I'm going to say very hurtful things, and I don't want to," Jocelyn replied.

I wished I could put my arm around her. Hold her in my lap. Kiss her slowly and reassure her with my body. But I couldn't do any of those things with our parents there. Jocelyn's eyelids were wet even though she'd squeezed them shut. I wanted to feed Hank his balls.

Hank shook his head and grumbled under his breath about "ingratitude."

My mother shrank small in her seat, openly crying, her hands over her still-flat belly.

I worked my hand over to Jocelyn's jeans and curled a finger in her belt loop, giving it a little tug, just so she knew I was there.

Jocelyn turned her head slightly in my direction and opened her eyes. Tears she'd been trying to hold back rolled down her cheeks, but she dashed them away quickly.

Honestly, the bus station couldn't come soon enough.

CHAPTER 22: GO, GO GREYHOUND

-Jacey-

My father ended up dropping us at a car rental agency, huffing and puffing over the Greyhound Bus Station having closed. We spent three-and-a-half awkward hours in the car, stopping at rest stops and gas stations only when Jeanie said she needed a break.

I would have rather peed my pants than ask my father for anything at that point. It was bad enough I'd cried. Caleb had been a love and kept his finger curled in my belt loop all the way to Thunder Bay.

"I suppose I'll have to pay for the car, too," my father grumbled, getting out of the Suburban.

Caleb stopped him. "Don't bother. I've got it covered. And don't expect to see us for a day or two. We need to cool off, and so do you."

My father glowered at Caleb, but it was best not to owe him anything. I guessed Caleb had discovered that, too.

"What's going on?" Jeanie asked from the truck.

"Caleb's decided he's a man, now. Even though he can't pay for his own college education," my father called back.

It was the wrong thing to say. Caleb gave my father a tight smile. I grabbed his elbow so he didn't punch my father in the face.

But it was so much worse. "I guess I'll have to get it from my father's estate that you've been mooching off all these years, then."

My father turned absolutely white. "I have done no such thing!"

"Good. Then there'll be more for me. Guess you're screwed, Mom. I hope you really love Hank because that's my money as much as it is yours, and I'm using it to become a doctor now. Guess you can't count on that little nest egg anymore," Caleb said, folding his arms.

"That's your mother's money—" Hank began.

"Actually, it's not. Hasn't been since I turned eighteen. Didn't you put an addition on the house last year? Maybe I should sue," Caleb replied flatly. "I'm done letting you dangle shit over my head. If it comes down to it, I'll pay for Jacey's education, too. You treat her like shit."

Jeanie looked distressed, her hands going over her belly again.

"Let's just go, Caleb," I said, tugging on his arm. "We can work all that out later when everybody's not angry."

Caleb glanced at his mother, sneered back at my father, then turned his back on the both of them.

"Don't you go upsetting your mother," my father yelled after us. "You call to tell us you're all right."

"Will do," Caleb agreed with a wave of his hand.

I felt a little relieved that we'd at least established that rule. Caleb bent down and grabbed both our packs, slinging one over each shoulder as we walked into the car rental place.

Half an hour later, we were in a small sedan, our packs in the back seat, Caleb driving. He'd chosen a stick shift once he learned I could drive one, too.

We traveled down the highway toward Grand Portage at the U.S./Canadian border. It was about an hour's drive, during which Caleb could finally put a hand on my thigh, and I could twine my fingers with his.

We weren't stopped at the border, simply flashed our passports and went on our way. I was surprised, however, when Caleb pulled off the road and drove into the Mt. Josephine rest stop.

"Caleb?" I asked when he parked as far from the facilities as possible.

"I need to touch you," Caleb said, his voice shaking with need.

I swallowed. "Sh-Should we go find a hotel?"

"Yes. But I need you now," Caleb replied. "I couldn't stand it in the Suburban with your father and my mother. Let me hold you, please?"

It was the "please" that did me in. "What do you want me to do?" I asked, examining the gear shift and the steering wheel. I just wasn't sure, in a car this size, if I was going to be able to squeeze into Caleb's lap.

"Get in the back seat," Caleb said. "Take off your pants and panties."

I bit my lip. "That's more than holding me, Caleb."

"Nobody's around. Please?" Caleb asked again. He ran his thumb under my lower lip, pulling it out from between my teeth.

I sighed and nodded. I'd missed his touch as well.

Caleb grabbed the back of my head and kissed me hard, hungrily. Then he backed off a bit to let me get out of the passenger seat.

Shaking with anticipation, I got in the back seat and leaned against the closed door so I could wriggle out of my pants and panties.

Caleb opened the opposite door just as I was finishing. He unzipped his pants, then climbed in the back seat and closed the door behind him.

His magnificent cock was already rigid, and I licked my lips just looking at it.

"How flexible are you?" Caleb asked, staring at me with hooded eyes filled with desire.

"Very," I replied, my voice husky.

"Can you get your ankles behind your head?" Caleb said.

I nodded. It was a party trick from when I was at sleepovers as a young girl, but I could still do it.

"Excellent. Do it," Caleb ordered.

I pulled my legs up and got my ankles to lock behind my head.

Caleb stared down at my exposed slit and gave me a slow smile. "You're so beautiful, Jacey. Everywhere."

My blush may have reached my mound, but I soon had no thoughts of embarrassment. I had no thoughts at all swimming around my head as Caleb leaned down and kissed my nether lips.

"Caleb..." I moaned.

Caleb flicked his tongue over my clit then settled in to deeply and truly pleasure me, sucking my clit while his fingers worked me to wetness.

It didn't take long for me to come around Caleb's fingers with a loud gasp. My legs might have come down and kicked Caleb, only he realized what my pleasure would do to me and gripped my legs to steady them while I shuddered.

Then the large head of him was at my entrance. "Baby, pull up your shirt. I want to see your breasts," Caleb said as he began easing his large cock into me.

I panted at the size of him. No matter how many times we did it, he always felt huge inside of me. With shaking hands, I lifted my shirt and freed my breasts from my bra so Caleb could look all he wanted.

My reward was the feel of his cock swelling impossibly more inside me.

"Caleb," I whimpered with need.

"Hold your legs up, baby," Caleb grunted, starting to thrust.

I wrapped my arms around my legs just to give some extra support. Caleb leaned his weight on his arms, his head swooping down to take a nipple in his mouth while he fucked me hard.

Little cries of pleasure issued from my throat, and Caleb swallowed them with his mouth when his lips fused to mine.

"I'm cumming inside, baby," Caleb whispered hotly in my ear as I felt my orgasm building.

I wouldn't have expected any less, but nodded against his cheek anyway.

After two more thrusts, I cried out as pleasure rolled over me. I felt myself tighten around Caleb's cock.

Caleb groaned then filled me with his hot cum, pushed all the way in me to the hilt.

I reached for Caleb, pulling him in for a satiated kiss.

"Mmm, baby you feel so good," Caleb sighed, keeping his cock buried inside me just a moment longer.

I laughed and combed my fingers through his hair. "We really should find a hotel."

"That's true. Otherwise I'll be ravaging you at every rest stop from here to Vermillion," Caleb chuckled. "Not that I'd mind…"

I swatted him. "Hotel. I don't want a park ranger tapping the window and telling us kids to put our clothes back on."

"Fair enough." Caleb gently pulled out of me, then fondled my nipple while he kissed me.

"Hotel!" I gasped a reprimand, as ready to go a second time as he was. But someone had to have some sense.

Caleb grumbled a protest but did his pants back up and helped me into mine.

He used my underwear—again—to clean me up, and put the panties in his back pocket.

I was going to have to see if Victoria's Secret offered lines of credit.

Looking mussed, Caleb crawled back out of the car and pulled me out after him. When he closed the door behind us, he pressed me against it for a steamy kiss.

"Caleb!" I breathed against his lips. "Hotel, hotel!"

"Good thing we told the parents we'd be a few days because we're not leaving that hotel for a while," Caleb muttered and stepped back, pulling his T-shirt out of his pants to hide his erection.

"Should we call them?" I asked, guilt pricking me a little, and not for the first time.

Caleb smoothed down the hair that had escaped my braid and shook his head. "Not until we're at the hotel. When I'm cock deep inside you. THEN we'll call."

"CALEB!" I gaped, scandalized.

Caleb gave me a wicked grin. "Wouldn't it be something, though?"

I thought he was joking. I hoped he was. He kissed my frown away then escorted me to the passenger side of the car and ushered me in.

Caleb got behind the wheel again, and while he drove, I found us a reasonably-priced motel near Grand Marais.

We parked outside an L-shaped, one-level, light gray, homey-looking motel. Caleb took our waterproof packs out of the trunk and hefted one over each shoulder once again, just grinning at me when I offered to take mine.

The motel office had wood-paneled walls and a great big moose head over the front desk. A flannel-wearing older man in suspenders with flyaway gray hair combed over a shiny bald center smiled at us as we entered.

"Hi, we'd like a room, please," Caleb said, setting our packs on the floor for the time being.

"Sure thing. How many nights?" the older gentleman asked. "And do you want a room with a kitchenette or...?"

"Could we have a room with just a queen bed? We'll figure out meals on our own," I said quickly, trying to make sure we chose the least costly room. Especially since Caleb would be paying for it.

Caleb raised an eyebrow and shook his head. "Kitchenette, please. And three nights, if you don't mind. We'd like to see a bit of the area."

"Caleb..." I whispered.

"Don't worry. I've got it covered," Caleb said, and kissed my temple.

The older gentleman at the desk chuckled. "My missus doesn't like spending money on the little luxuries, either. Don't you worry, honey. It's not that much more for the kitchenette."

I sighed and let Caleb pay for the upgraded room. But I did pick up my own bag this time before Caleb could.

"Ooo, boy, you'd better watch yourself. You've got a feisty one there," the older gentleman laughed.

"Don't I know it," Caleb replied, though more to himself than to the desk clerk.

Once I got outside, of course, I had no idea which way I was going, since I hadn't seen the room number on the key. A real deadbolt key.

Caleb took my hand firmly and marched us in the direction of the room with the kitchenette—Room 3, as it turned out.

"Don't be mad, please?" Caleb asked, the cutest puppy-dog expression on his face. "I really want us to have a nice time, and if we have a kitchenette—"

"There's more surfaces for us to have sex on?" I scoffed.

Caleb paused a beat outside our door then burst out laughing. "Well, yeah, that, too, but I was thinking I could cook for you. We might be able to save money on meals."

Oh God. I knew I was blushing to the roots of my hair, and there was nothing I could do about it. I wished the ground would swallow me whole.

"I like your thinking, though," Caleb smirked at me.

"Yeah, well, you only THINK you're getting lucky," I huffed, pushing past him once the door was open. I stomped into the bedroom with its one queen-sized bed and dropped my bag by the wood-paneled wall. There was something charming about the rustic nature of the place, but I was busy being angry at Caleb. Or maybe just embarrassed at myself. Or something.

Caleb plopped his bag in a chair and walked up behind me, wrapping his arms around my waist. "Baby, don't be like that," he begged, nuzzling my neck.

I wasn't even entirely sure why I was being "like that" anymore. I pouted and peeked up at Caleb. "I really did research this motel."

"I know, baby. I'm sorry. I just wanted to do a little upgrade. It's a great motel, and very reasonably priced," Caleb reassured me.

I pouted a moment longer, then gave in with a sigh. "I don't suppose I'd be able to lie next to you all night in that bed and NOT have sex."

"That's my baby," Caleb murmured. He slid his hand down past the waistband of my pants. "Let me make it up to you."

CHAPTER 23: CALLING HOME

-Caleb-

My Jacey was wet for me as I slowly curled my fingers inside her, and I groaned, imagining the feel of that warm, tight wetness around my dick. But this was about her, not me, and even if I died of blue balls, I was going to pleasure the fuck out of her before thinking of opening my pants. Well, all right, I'd think about it, but I wouldn't do it. Not yet.

I thumbed her swollen clit as I kissed along her neck. She leaned, boneless, against me.

"Caleb," Jocelyn whispered, and the sound of my name on her lips, spoken that needy way, made my balls tighten.

"Mhm?" I pulled the collar of her shirt aside with my free hand and nibbled her shoulder.

Anything she might have said to me was lost in a moan, and I felt her juices drip over my fingers as she came hard against my hand.

"So eager," I murmured as I nuzzled the shell of her ear.

"You made me this way," Jocelyn accused me, panting, clinging to my arm just to stay upright.

I chuckled. "And I'm not a bit sorry." I pulled my hand out of her pants and licked my fingers. Fuck me, but she always tasted so good.

Jocelyn started wobbling toward the living room, but I caught her around the waist and dumped her on the bed.

"Who said I was done with you?" I asked, arching my eyebrow.

"You have a one-track mind," Jocelyn smiled.

"I do when it comes to you. Not gonna apologize for that, either." I pulled off her shoes and socks then unzipped her pants and peeled those off her as well.

Jocelyn widened her legs for me, clearly expecting me to go in balls deep, but I had another agenda right now.

I tugged Jocelyn to the edge of the bed and tossed her legs over my shoulders.

Jocelyn knew where I was going with this, and she gasped and threaded her fingers through my hair just as I buried my tongue in her body. "Caleb..."

Fuck me. There should be a licorice flavor called "Jacey." I feasted to my heart's content, making her come twice, and was rather proud of that fact.

"Caleb," Jocelyn moaned, shaking, tugging my hair. "Be inside me, PLEASE!"

I gave her clit one last, slow lick, then stood. "Who can say no to an invitation like that?"

As Jocelyn shimmied out of her shirt and bra, I tossed my shirt, pants, and boxers into the bedroom's great unknown. My dick was like a divining rod, pointing straight at her center.

Jocelyn held out her arms to me, and I got on the bed on top of her, easing into her until our hips met. She was so wet, it was hard not to go straight in to the hilt in one thrust. But that wasn't the kind of love I wanted to make today.

Wrapping her arms and legs around me, Jocelyn peppered the sweetest kisses over my skin. I wanted to ride her hard and fast until both of us were satisfied, but instead, I slowly rocked my hips against hers, loving on her body as I did so.

Her breasts were big and firm and jiggled naturally with the rocking. I had to stare. My mouth went dry with the desire to touch and suck on them. So I did.

"Caleb..." Jocelyn panted, clinging to me. "Caleb... m-more..."

I was just about to comply when a thought struck me. I gave Jocelyn a wicked smile and reached onto the bedside table for my phone.

Her eyes widened when she realized what I was going to do. "Caleb, no, that's—"

I rolled my hips, and she went almost cross-eyed, whatever protest she'd been about to make dying on her lips.

Meanwhile, I scrolled through my contacts until I found Hank's number. "Hank, how's it going?" I asked, trapping the phone between my ear and my shoulder while I twiddled Jocelyn's nipples.

She bit her lip and gave me a look that promised sweet revenge later.

"Where are you two?" Hank demanded.

"Just outside Grand Marais. Not to worry. I'm taking good care of Jacey," I replied, pumping my cock into her harder and faster.

Jocelyn trembled with the effort not to make any noise.

"You'd better be," Hank said. "And I'll expect you home by tomorrow."

"No can do," I responded, starting to pant myself. "I'm afraid I booked three nights here so Jacey and I can see the sights."

Hank growled. "What are you doing right now?"

"Hiking. Working up quite a sweat, actually," I said, grinning down at Jocelyn. I knew it was unfair, but I moved my hand in to thumb her clit, causing her to detonate around me and bite back a scream of pleasure.

"What was that?" Hank asked.

"Jacey just tripped over a rock. She's fine," I gasped, emptying my cum into her body.

"Can't believe you've got Jacey hiking. She's never shown any interest in that before," Hank grunted.

I had to swallow several times before answering, I was panting so hard in the aftermath. "I guess she just never found the right companion."

"Whatever," Hank said dismissively. "I want you two back sometime tomorrow. That's not negotiable."

"Hmm..." I murmured, massaging Jocelyn's breast while she came down. "I'm going to have to go with 'no.' I know that's a word you're not used to hearing, but..."

"Caleb! You do as I say!" Hank snarled.

"B'bye," I replied, ending the call.

Jocelyn scowled at me, but her expression lightened when I kissed her nose.

"I can't believe you did that," she said. "I thought you were kidding before!"

"I was, and then I wasn't. That's just how it went," I grinned.

"Do you plan to give all your updates while we're going at it?" Jocelyn sniffed.

I pretended to think about it.

Jocelyn swatted me. "You'd better not!"

I laughed and kissed her. "I just couldn't resist."

"Well, resist next time," Jocelyn groused.

I kissed her again and nuzzled her neck. "Okay, baby. Whatever you want."

Jocelyn sighed in defeat and draped her arms around my neck. "You know what I want."

Still cock deep in her with a semi, I grinned and rolled my hips.

I gave Jocelyn what we both wanted twice more, until my balls were completely empty and she was sobbing with pleasure.

Then I slid my overworked cock out of her body and got up, feeling completely sated. "I'll be back, baby. You just relax," I said.

Jocelyn nodded tiredly.

I went to the bathroom and drew a bath in the small tub. Then I went back to the bed and scooped Jocelyn up in my arms.

"Mmm?" Jocelyn asked, already half asleep.

"I thought you might like a bath after all our fun today," I smiled, lowering her gently into the tub.

Jocelyn groaned as the warm water washed over her skin. She leaned back, and I kissed her forehead.

Jocelyn reached for a little wrapped soap, but I beat her to it. "Just relax, baby," I murmured, unwrapping the soap. I dipped my hands into the water, lathered them up with soap, and began washing my Jacey gently.

I'll admit to being a bit naughty—I was a red-blooded man whose woman was naked in the bath—and her breasts and vaginal area got very, VERY clean while she writhed against my hands. But aside from a little fingering, I tried to be good.

Jocelyn pulled my head down to kiss me when I finished rinsing her clean, and I began fingering her in earnest until she cried out against my lips.

"That's my baby," I grinned. She was absolutely boneless when I undid her hair and took the little shampoo from the edge of the tub, encouraging her to lay back in the water with her legs folded up so I could wash her hair.

I ran the thick locks slowly through my fingers, enjoying the feel of her finally free hair. I, of course, imagined fucking her with her thick hair fanned out over the pillows. Or, better still, Jocelyn riding me while her hair hung around us like a curtain. It was so soft, too. Impossible not to touch.

"Caleb?" Jocelyn asked after a while, and I realized I'd just been running my fingers through her hair for several minutes.

"Your hair is amazing, baby. Sorry, I'll wash it now," I said. I put shampoo on my hands and began massaging it into her scalp, then soaped her hair all the way down to the ends.

Jocelyn hummed happily, and I gave her scalp some extra, unnecessary massaging before rinsing out the shampoo and moving on to conditioner.

"Caleb, you're really good at this," Jocelyn sighed.

"Practice makes perfect," I said evasively.

"You had another girlfriend with long hair," Jocelyn inferred.

I wasn't going to lie to her. "Yes. Two."

"At... the same time?" Jocelyn asked cautiously.

I chuckled at how hard she was trying not to offend me. "I only have one girlfriend at a time, Jacey. And I wasn't seeing anyone when we became lovers."

"Oh. Good. Me, neither," Jocelyn said, her cheeks pink.

"I kind of figured. Though that still boggles my mind," I responded. "I always assumed the high school boys were going to be all over you. College, too, for that matter." I frowned, remembering Jocelyn was attending her first year of college this year. And there would be boys. Boys with their eyes on her.

Jocelyn reached up and cupped my cheek. "You don't need to worry about any college boys. They're just boys. You're a man. Plus, I love you. Nobody can compete with that."

I relaxed and rinsed the conditioner out of Jocelyn's hair. "I don't throw the 'L' word out to just anybody, either. I only said it to my first college girlfriend. She ended up cheating on me with the captain of the football team, so I'm more careful now."

"You said you loved me, though," Jocelyn said with a soft smile.

I got Jocelyn sitting up and kissed her thoroughly. "That's because I do love you."

Jocelyn beamed at me.

"Let's get you out of the tub before you get all prune-y," I suggested, and helped Jocelyn to her feet. I wrapped a towel around her and carried her back to the bed.

"You really are spoiling me rotten," Jocelyn warned me with a soft smile on her face.

"You deserve it," I said. I looked over the side of the bed at her purple waterproof sack. "Mind if I dig in your bag for your hairbrush?"

Jocelyn blushed, but nodded. "Just ignore the Care Bear underwear."

I grinned. "Are you kidding? I'm stealing that off you next."

"Pretty soon, I won't have any panties to wear at all," Jocelyn complained.

I winked at her. "I'm not seeing a problem with this."

Jocelyn snorted but let me climb over the side of the bed and ransack her bag. The Care Bear undies were adorable. I was definitely going to beg her to wear them for me.

My hand hit on her hairbrush and a comb. I took a binder off the handle of the hairbrush and put it around my wrist.

Then I sat up and snuggled up behind Jocelyn. "You have beautiful hair."

"Thanks," Jocelyn said, blushing again.

I started gently brushing it from the ends up. I placed a kiss on Jocelyn's bare shoulder when I got to her mid-back. "Shame to tie it back, but if we want to go out walking, probably best in case it's windy."

"Do you know how to braid?" Jocelyn asked me, turning her head.

"I do," I replied proudly. I followed up my words with a demonstration, even going with a fancy French braid.

Jocelyn snuggled into my lap, her smile content. "I'm glad we're not going home right away."

"Me, too," I said. "Honestly, your dad can take a flying leap."

"I'm worried about what he'll do," Jocelyn responded quietly.

I shrugged. "Whatever it is, you have me. I wasn't kidding when I said I'd pay for your education if I need to. I don't want him manipulating you into being a nanny."

"Is it really so bad of them to ask us to help out?" Jocelyn whispered, looking up at me with vulnerable eyes.

"Yes," I said firmly. "They shouldn't be having a kid if they can't take care of it themselves. You're eighteen, Jacey. You deserve everything that implies."

"Including an older boyfriend?" Jocelyn teased.

I kissed her, and slipped my hand inside her towel to massage her breast. "Especially that."

CHAPTER 24: GRAND MARAIS

-JACEY-

The lavender freshness of the bath didn't last long, and neither did the braid. Oh, we'd had every intention of going out to see the sights Grand Marais and the North Shore of Lake Superior had to offer, but instead, I'd ended up staring at the ceiling fan while Caleb ravaged me again. Not that I'd had much time to examine the 1990s-style fan. I was too busy enjoying the sex.

If Caleb and I ever had a honeymoon, it would be unreal.

I slept next to Caleb, his arm draped over my belly. I was happily sound asleep when Caleb started to tremble, then thrash.

"No..." he groaned. "No..."

"Caleb," I said quickly, catching his face between my hands. "Caleb, wake up! You're having a bad dream!"

Caleb panted and leaned over me, slapping on the light on the bedside table. "Jacey?"

"Yeah. I'm here." My bare breasts pressed against his back as I hugged him from behind when he sat up.

Caleb turned and began touching my face and the back of my head, his hands clammy with cold sweat. "Jacey... fuck... Jesus..."

"Was it that man again?" I asked, putting my hands over his when he rested his palms on my cheeks.

Caleb shook his head, squeezing his eyes shut with a shudder. "This time... it was you."

"Oh... Caleb," I whispered. I cuddled into his lap and held him in my arms. "I'm okay, see? Nothing broken."

Caleb ran his hands over the rest of me then pressed his forehead to my shoulder with relief. "Fuck, that was the most horrible thing I've ever fucking seen. I bashed your head in!"

I combed my fingers through his hair. "You didn't. You never would. I'm here. I love you. Everything is fine." I was beginning to wonder if maybe we should go to the authorities just for Caleb's peace of mind.

When I felt the smallest trickle of a cooling tear over my skin, that settled it for me. "Caleb, I think we should go to the police."

"The police?" Caleb repeated, his head coming up.

"It's really been bothering you, what happened. I think... maybe if you had some closure?" I suggested.

Caleb stared at me for a long time. "What about the loggers?"

"What are they going to be able to do? We're in America now," I said. I stroked Caleb's cheek. "I'll do anything, Caleb. Anything to help you feel better. Even face the loggers and the law and everything."

Caleb gave me a nervous smile and a kiss. "Baby, I don't want anything to happen to you." He shifted us so I was straddling him and eased his thick cock into me. "This is all I need. I promise."

I had to give the man credit. He was good at sidetracking me. But two could play that game. He needed more than sex with the woman he loved. He knew it. I knew it. It was simply my job to get him to make peace with it.

I let Caleb move my hips against his, bracing myself on his chest. As always, he watched my breasts jiggle while he helped me ride him.

"Caleb," I panted, "I'm not going to let this go..."

"Mhm," Caleb replied, hitting my G spot.

The man didn't play fair! I threw my head back and moaned.

"That's it. Give it to me, baby," Caleb hissed, pushing up into me.

I gave it to him. Anything and everything he wanted. He guided my hips at just the right angle, rubbing in just the right places. I sobbed as I came hard, shuddering on top of him.

Caleb gripped my hips, burying himself deep inside me when he came as well.

While usually feeling Caleb's hot cum in me gave me a sense of triumph, now it gave me the slightest sense of defeat. Caleb had managed to distract me from an important conversation.

Even though Caleb was still cock deep in me, I took a deep breath and mustered my reserves, determined not to be sidetracked this time. "Caleb, we need to go to the police."

Caleb groaned, his lips closing over one of my nipples. He lapped it with his tongue and played with it with his teeth, and I couldn't stop myself from making a needy sound.

His cock was perking up again inside me, and it would be easy, so easy, to let him fuck me absolutely senseless.

No, I decided. No, I was going to get my point across. I wouldn't let him distract me again!

"Caleb," I said sharply, tugging on his hair so he let go of my nipple with a soft "pop." "I mean it. We need to go to the police. You need closure, and it's the right thing to do. Having sex with me for three days, while fantastic, is still not going to make the nightmares go away. Please."

Caleb looked down at me. He ran his fingers through my loose hair and caressed my cheek with his thumb. "Before you just wanted to let it go."

"Before I was scared of the loggers, and I didn't want you to get into trouble." I swallowed as he began rocking gently, slipping his cock in and out, but not in such a way as we couldn't hold a conversation. "Before… before I didn't realize what it was going to do to you. Please, Caleb. I want to at least try."

"Okay, baby." Caleb gave me a nervous half-smile, but I took his words as a promise just the same.

Caleb rolled me underneath him, both of us getting lost in the sex once more.

I wrapped my arms around the back of his neck and closed my eyes as Caleb had me, slow and sweet. He massaged my ass as he pumped his cock into me, and I wrapped my legs around his waist.

We came together this time, me cresting the wave of my orgasm as he spilled his hot cum into me.

Then we just held each other, both afraid to burst the bubble.

"Shower," Caleb finally said sadly. "We need to shower before we go to the police."

I nodded and kissed him, stroking his hair. "It's the right thing to do. And it might help."

"I hope so," Caleb replied. He very gently pulled his dick from my body and rolled off the bed. "I'll go first. If we go in there together, we'll never leave."

I laughed a little. "True."

Caleb gave me that same, nervous half-smile, then went into the bathroom.

I got up and busied myself setting out clothes for the both of us. It was the wee hours of the morning, but I was pretty sure any police station would be open for a murder confession.

And, I noted, I really was running low on underwear. In fact, I had no idea where my semi-acceptable panties had gone. I just had two pairs of my Care Bear underwear left.

I plucked one pair out of my drawer, wondering where, exactly, Caleb was hoarding my panties.

When I had clothes laid out for both of us, Caleb came out of the bathroom with a towel modestly wrapped around his waist. Pity.

As though reading my thoughts, Caleb smirked. "You'd better go shower yourself, little miss naked. If you want us to go to the police station."

"No, we're going," I said firmly. I sashayed past him and went into the bathroom.

Within forty-five minutes, Caleb and I were in the car and on our way to the Cook County Sheriff.

Caleb kept his hand on my leg the entire way, even though it wasn't far. I twined my fingers with his.

Ten silent minutes brought us to the Sheriff's Department. Caleb and I sat in the parking lot, staring at the red brick building for some time.

Then I reached up and stroked Caleb's cheek. "It's time."

Caleb nodded, and the two of us got out of the car. Caleb handed me the keys to the car and the motel room. "You never know," he said softly.

'You never know if I'm going to be detained,' was what he meant. In fact, now that I thought about it, that was a very real possibility.

I stood, frozen on the spot until Caleb tugged my hand with a sad smile. "It'll be okay, baby. One foot in front of the other."

I trudged with Caleb to the door then went inside. We went to the front desk holding hands.

"Hi," Caleb said to the officer working the desk.

The officer looked up, blinking owlishly at us. It was still pretty early. "Yes?"

"I've... come to report a crime. A murder," Caleb went on after clearing his throat a few times.

That perked the officer right up. "Pierson—hey, PIERSON—we've got a young man here wanting to report a murder—what is your name, son?"

"Caleb Killeen," Caleb responded.

"I'm Jacey—er, Jocelyn—Collins. It was murder in defense of another. Me," I said quickly before anyone started getting any ideas.

The officer flicked his eyes over Caleb. "Are you the perpetrator?"

"Yes, sir," Caleb replied.

"When and where did this murder occur?" another officer, I assumed to be Pierson, asked, coming up to the front.

"About a week ago around Shimmer Lake, Ontario," Caleb said.

"Ontario? A week ago? You didn't think to report it to the Mounties?" Pierson pressed.

"We were threatened, sir," I explained.

"Threatened? By whom?" Pierson asked.

"There was this illegal logging operation we kind of stumbled upon right after the incident, and they didn't want their location to be revealed," I said.

"Bailey, we're going to need some coffees," Pierson called behind him. "You two are going to need to come with me."

Caleb and I both nodded and started after Pierson. When Bailey came with the coffees, Pierson jerked his head in the direction of a door. "Put this little lady in there. I'll talk with her separately in a bit."

I must have shown some distress on my face because Pierson smiled kindly at me. "I'm not going to waterboard your boyfriend. Just sit tight."

"Okay," I replied with uncertainty. Bailey showed me into a room with a table and a couple of chairs I realized must be an "interrogation" room. Though I was pretty sure they called them "interview" rooms now, and this one didn't seem so scary.

I sat down, and Bailey placed a cup in front of me. "Can I see your ID, Miss Collins?" he asked kindly, settling across from me.

I dug out my driver's license and my passport and handed them over.

"Well, this is some happy birthday to you," Bailey grunted, looking over my information.

"Tell me about it," I sighed.

CHAPTER 25: WHATEVER HAPPENED TO BILL?

-CALEB-

All things being equal, I'd have rather been back at the motel having sex therapy with Jocelyn. As it was, I was now sitting at a table across from Pierson, who had taken out a recording device and a notepad.

"Mr. Killeen, do you mind if I record this conversation?" Pierson asked.

"Go right ahead," I replied.

Pierson turned on the recorder and said the date and the crime in question. Then he looked at me. "Please state your name for the record."

"Caleb Killeen," I responded clearly.

"And you're sure you don't want an attorney present?" Pierson asked.

I shook my head. "Not at this time, thank you. I'd just like to get this off my chest."

"Fair enough. So, Miss Collins was saying you killed a man in defense of another. Her?" Pierson said.

I nodded. "Yes, sir. Bill shot at me and winged me on the side of the head." I gestured to the spot that was still an angry red. "I fell to the ground. I think he must have thought I was dead, but he went chasing Jacey through the woods, and when I got to her, he'd cornered her against a tree and what he was saying..."

"What was he saying?" Pierson asked.

I shuddered. "I don't remember the words exactly, but he intended to r-rape her. Probably kill her after."

"So... what did you do then?" Pierson prodded.

"I picked up a rock and surprised him from behind. I bashed in his skull." I scrubbed my hands over my face, trying to make the image go away.

Pierson kept taking notes. "Did he still have a gun?"

"Yes, sir. Shotgun. I don't know anything more than that—I'm not familiar with types of guns," I admitted.

"That's okay. Let's back up a little bit. How did you come across this man?" Pierson asked.

I gave a short history of our situation, starting from the family fishing trip to the fight we'd had with Hank to the storm. "I wish I could tell you where we ended up. There were a lot of rocks. I don't think many fishermen go that way because of the rocks."

"Um... just to clarify... Miss Collins is your sister?" Pierson inquired delicately.

"Stepsister. We're not related," I said quickly.

"I was going to say, you seemed rather close for... brother and sister. Closer than a brother and sister are supposed to be," Pierson went on.

"It just kinda... happened. It's a long story. She had a crush on me, I pushed her away, she grew up, I grew up..." I tried to explain.

"Son, I've seen her. You don't need to explain," Pierson chuckled.

I scowled.

Pierson held up his hands. "I've also seen how supportive she is of you. You're a very lucky man."

"Our parents don't know, so if we could keep it that way, that'd be great," I said.

"You're a grown adult, Mr. Killeen. So is Miss Collins. There's no crime there, and nothing for me to report," Pierson replied.

I sagged back in my chair with relief. "Thanks."

"You're welcome. Now, keep going. I'd like to get the full picture," Pierson said.

"Okay. The canoe overturned, and Jacey hit her head. She was out cold. I dragged her to the only piece of land I could see and got us up over the rocks. That was not a fun experience in socks, let me tell you," I continued.

"I'd like to take some pictures. May I?" Pierson asked.

I nodded and stood. Pierson took out a phone and took a picture of the side of my head. I also showed him my shins and my feet, still angry and a bit cut up from the rocks and the walking overland in my socks.

"Thank you, Mr. Killeen," Pierson said.

I sat back down and waited for more questions.

"How did you happen upon... Bill? Do you know his full name?" Pierson asked.

"No. Just Bill. And we learned that from the loggers. He never gave us his name," I said.

"Well, hopefully the Mounties will be able to find these loggers. I take it you didn't stay exposed on the shoreline?" Pierson continued.

"No. We decided we needed to get to shelter. That's how the trouble started. We found one of those cabins that Jacey once told me were 'grandfathered in' by the Canadian government. It seemed to be empty—no, it WAS empty until Bill came. He surprised us when we were coming back from having a bath," I explained. "He first told us to clear off. Then he saw Jacey and... changed his mind. I told her to run. He shot at me."

"How did he change his mind?" Pierson asked.

My jaw worked, the white-hot rage from that moment washing over me again. "He asked if that was 'a woman' and said maybe we owed him for his hospitality. I filled in the blanks. I told her to run."

"And he had his gun pointed at you when he made that demand?" Pierson inferred.

"Yes," I said.

Pierson nodded. "I think Miss Collins was very lucky to have you around."

"... Thanks," I mumbled.

"And after you killed Bill?" Pierson asked.

"Jacey and I decided we needed to find some kind of road, in case Bill had friends. We couldn't wait around to be found anymore. I mean, we were there for two days without a peep. I even tried spelling out 'HELP' with rocks on the shoreline, but with the rocks just past it, you'd have needed a helicopter to see it," I said.

"You did find the road, though." Pierson was taking notes on his notepad.

"We did. We heard a logging truck. If there's a logging truck, you know there's going to be a road," I continued.

"You thought you were saved," Pierson murmured sympathetically.

I laughed, and it was all bitterness. "We weren't. It was an illegal logging operation. They only gave first names, too. I don't even remember what they were. We were scared shitless. They were talking about killing us, then they threw us in a shed for two days. At least there was food and clothes in there."

"Obviously, they didn't kill you," Pierson said.

"They knocked us out with some kind of chemicals. When we woke up, we were at the old fly-in camp across from our campsite," I went on. "There was a representative from the Natural Resources department there, and he looked us over and decided we were okay. So Hank decided to just continue our trip like nothing happened."

"You didn't report the murder or the illegal loggers at the time," Pierson stated.

"They left a note that we burned at the fly-in camp saying how much we were going to regret it if we said anything. They also took care of Bill's body, I think. He was a friend of theirs," I said.

"So... you don't know exactly where you were, and you're fairly certain there is now no body to find..." Pierson concluded.

My shoulders slumped. "That's basically it, yeah."

"You're a good man, coming in anyway," Pierson said. "You could just have never reported this crime, and there would never have been an investigation or anything."

"We're still not sure what the loggers are going to do to us, but Jacey thought if I got some closure, it might help my mental state," I replied.

"Mental state?" Pierson echoed.

"I've been having nightmares," I explained.

"Ah. That's to be expected. We'll get you some counseling resources around where you live," Pierson said.

I stared at him. "I'm not... going to prison?"

"Nope. I'll go ahead and file this with the district attorney and get the report up to our Canadian friends, but as long as Miss Collins's story matches yours, there is no need to take this any further," Pierson replied. "It was a horrible thing, but it sounds like it was necessary."

"Okay," I said quietly. "Okay, thanks."

"Thank you. Not a lot of people in your shoes would come to report a crime just because it was morally right to do so," Pierson praised me. "Now, I imagine the Mounties might start looking for your illegal logging operation. If it seems like they're going to give you trouble, you go to the authorities, okay?"

I nodded. "Yes, sir."

"I'm just going to go make some calls and interview Miss Collins. You sit tight. I'm filing this report with the district attorney, but I honestly don't see it going anywhere. I'll probably know within the hour, okay?" Pierson said kindly.

"Thank you, sir," I replied.

Pierson stopped the recording and picked up the recorder and his notes, put his phone in his pocket, and headed out the door.

I closed my eyes, missing Jocelyn. Her solid presence was already a pillar holding up my life, and that shocked and scared me in equal measure. I'd never had a girlfriend become so entrenched in the bedrock of my life, not even my first college girlfriend who had broken my heart.

It was probably all the trauma we'd muddled through together, I reasoned. Maybe when things died down, I'd be less dependent on her, and she'd be less dependent on me, and we could take things slow like a normal couple.

Then I remembered the sweet way she'd given her body to me under the stars, the sweet kisses, the laughter, and the snuggling, and the way she held me when I'd had a nightmare. Nope, I very much doubted we were going to be able to take it slow at this point.

After an hour or two, Pierson showed up again with a woman I didn't recognize.

"Mr. Killeen, this is District Attorney Amanda Nelson. She's been negotiating with the Canadian government on your behalf," Pierson said.

Ms. Nelson held out her hand, and I took it tentatively. "Um... hi?"

"Mr. Killeen, the Canadian authorities are prepared to drop any and all charges against you and Miss Collins—" Ms. Nelson began.

"Wait, why would there be any charges against Jacey?" I asked.

"Conspiracy to cover up a crime. Don't worry, a good barrister in Canada will make that go away in a day. I just thought it would be easier if you and Miss Collins could go back to Canada, to Shimmer Lake, and try to help the Canadian authorities find the illegal logging operation," Ms. Nelson said.

I blinked at her. "So, if Jacey and I go back to Canada and help find the illegal logging operation, this all goes away?"

"It becomes a report in a file in a box in a warehouse," Ms. Nelson said with a nod.

"I'll have to talk with Jacey about it," I responded after a pause.

"Of course. We'll have her brought in here so you can make a decision," Ms. Nelson assured me.

Pierson and Ms. Nelson left, and Bailey returned scant minutes later with Jocelyn.

Jocelyn immediately pulled the opposite chair up next to me and leaned her head on my shoulder. "Did it all go okay? Are you all right?"

"Yeah," I said. "You?"

"Yeah." Jocelyn took my hand and threaded her fingers through mine. "Pierson said there's no reason to tell our parents anything about the murder. We can just go back to Shimmer Lake and help the authorities find those assholes who were going to kill us."

"Those assholes might still try to kill us if we help catch them, Jacey," I reminded her.

Jocelyn squeezed my hand. "I don't want to live in fear, Caleb. They're always going to be dangling in the background if we don't stop them."

"True." I turned my head and kissed her temple. "You're sure this is okay? With you?"

"Yeah. We'll go up and come back, maybe in time to continue our reservation at the motel," Jocelyn suggested.

I grinned at that. "Sounds like a plan. Let's let the motel owner know we'll be gone a couple of days at the most and extend our stay a bit."

"Okay. Because I still want to see Grand Marais with you," Jocelyn said.

I gave her a light kiss on the lips. "Me, too."

CHAPTER 26: LOOKING FOR LOGGERS

-Jacey-

The boat skimmed over the water as Caleb and I sat on the middle seat. There was a conservation officer in front of us and two Mounties behind in the boat.

A helicopter had been thrown around as an idea, but ultimately, the Mounties hadn't wanted to scare the loggers off.

The conservation officer had taken our description of the terrain and the cabin and decided we had probably gone past Little Shimmer in the storm to a little pocket of a lake called Devil's Mouth. He eagerly informed us of how good the fishing was there, provided you could get in and out. Getting in and out was the problem. Not even the conservation officers went there—not even on a sunny day.

Fortunately, or perhaps unfortunately, for us, this old-timer had absolutely no fear and regaled us with stories of every nook and cranny of Shimmer, Little Shimmer, and the various portages and tiny lakes around them.

"Christ, man, how did you all even learn about this lake?!" one of the Mounties finally said from the back of the boat as he tried to navigate through a minefield of rocks.

"Oh, back about forty years ago, water in the lakes was as high as it's ever been, and a couple of fishermen managed to get back there. When they told the others about their haul, well, real fishermen follow the fish, son. Not many a soul would brave the area now, but that spring, they were coming out of here with buckets of big fish. Buckets," the older conservation officer said.

The Mounties looked at us. "How did you even get back here?"

"We had a canoe. With a motor, but... well, those are probably destroyed or sunk or something by now," Caleb answered.

"Did you really go walkin' through the woods naked?" the conservation officer chortled.

I blushed, and Caleb put an arm around me, life jacket and all. "We didn't have much of a choice after the wind blew our clothes away."

"I'd have paid good money to see that. Not to besmirch your modesty, young lady, just to see two people walkin' around the woods naked in September. It'd be a rarer sight than Bigfoot," the conservation officer said.

The boat hit a rock, and the conservation officer frowned. "Do you two need me to come back there and drive?!"

"I'd like to see you try it, old man!" a frustrated Mountie shot back.

"Then get out of my way, whipper snapper," the conservation officer barked.

The Mountie who had been running the motor switched places with the conservation officer.

"Caleb, Jacey," the conservation officer said authoritatively. "Get out them paddles. You two at least have some experience, not like this landlubber."

I stifled a laugh and picked up one of the oars. Caleb picked up the other, and we very slowly navigated through the rocks, Caleb occasionally giving a little push on one side when the conservation officer called out, me on the other.

It didn't take long before he didn't even have to tell us what to do. As the conservation officer did his best to get us through without hitting anything, Caleb and I bumped and prodded the nose of the boat between the harder passings.

The Mountie at the front of the boat looked embarrassed while his partner couldn't stop snickering.

"Don't laugh. We have to get back out of here, too," the Mountie at the front of the boat grumped.

That made the other Mountie go quiet.

Eventually, we made it to the mouth of a very small lake. Rocks rose on all sides. There didn't seem to be a safe berth to tie the boat to.

"Oh, that's promising," the conservation officer said, pointing to one side of the lake.

Bobbing listlessly between the rock and the shoreline was my purple life jacket.

"Yeah, that's mine," I confirmed.

Caleb was alert and looking around. "The shore we ended up on should have 'HELP' spelled out in rocks unless the loggers got rid of it."

"How would anyone even see that from here?" the Mountie in front snorted.

"Good thinking, son, but the landlubber is right. We're not going to be able to see that from behind the rest of the rocks here," the conservation officer said.

"Thanks," the landlubber in question grumbled.

The conservation officer navigated the boat close to one shoreline, bumping the nose between two rocks. "All right, landlubber, time to earn your keep. I'll keep running the motor and keep the boat here. You go up and see if you can find anything."

The Mountie groaned but dutifully got out of the boat and carefully picked his way over jagged rocks to investigate the shoreline. "No, nothing here. Not enough loose rock to make a 'HELP' sign, no signs of activity."

"Well, then, get back in the boat," the conservation officer said.

The Mountie was even more careful getting back, and let out an audible sigh of relief once he was back on the front bench.

The conservation officer chuckled. "You're just going to have to do it again. I'd keep holding your breath."

The other Mountie tried to cover an explosion of laughter with a cough.

We took Devil's Teeth in a circle, the Mountie getting out periodically to check the shoreline again. Once we were about three-quarters of the way around, the Mountie stopped as soon as he got past the rocks and let out a whistle.

"Does that mean we should get out?" Caleb asked.

"You're our best bet at finding the landmarks," the other Mountie said. He crawled to the front of the boat and began carefully walking across the rocks himself.

"I'll stay here and wait for you to come back," the conservation officer reassured us. "I'd come, too, but there's nowhere to tie off the boat."

"So, just the four of us are going to go up against a bunch of big, burly guys with guns?" Caleb asked, incredulous as I was.

One of the Mounties flashed us his sidearm. "Also, as soon as we find the loggers, we're setting down a GPS device and getting the hell out of Dodge. You don't need to be there for that. You just need to get us to the road."

I swallowed. "Okay."

Caleb and I then tiptoed over the rocks and the conservation officer moved back a little so the nose of the boat wasn't bumping rock anymore.

There, on the ground, was still spelled out Caleb's 'HELP' sign.

"So, let's go to this cabin first. I figure that's the first landmark," the 'landlubber' Mountie said.

Caleb led the way to the cabin with a Mountie right behind him. I walked in the middle while the other Mountie took up the rear.

I had to give credit to Caleb's memory—we arrived at the cabin without veering in the wrong direction once.

Our little love nest looked just as unassuming as it always had. The Mountie in the lead motioned for Caleb to get behind him and opened the door.

A god-awful smell rolled out of the cabin, and we all coughed and covered our faces.

The Mountie did a quick look around the inside, then shut the door again. "Suffice to say, the body was moved."

"Moved?" Caleb repeated.

The Mountie nodded. "It's on the bed."

I shuddered. I'd lost my virginity on that bed.

Caleb must have had a similar thought, because he put an arm around me.

"Well, we might as well leave our life jackets here. We don't want them blowing away like yours did, and this is the only landmark we've got so far," the first Mountie said.

It was a bit morbid, but he had a point. We all took off our life jackets.

"Where to from here?" one of the Mounties asked.

"I ran into the woods. I didn't really have a direction," I admitted.

The other Mountie knelt on the ground and looked into the woods, examining the earth and the pine needles. "I think they left enough evidence for us to follow." He unclipped a walkie-talkie from his belt. "You two stay here. We'll radio if we need you."

"Okay," Caleb said, taking the walkie-talkie.

The two Mounties walked slowly into the trees, following clues only they could see.

Caleb sat down on a bed of pine needles and gestured for me to sit in his lap.

I did and curled my head under his chin. Caleb kissed my hair and took both my hands, threading his fingers through mine.

"This doesn't diminish anything that happened here," Caleb assured me. "I will NEVER forget how you gave yourself to me under the shooting stars."

I nodded and squeezed Caleb's hands. "I won't ever forget it, either. Even if Bill is... currently... um... stinking up the place."

I must have looked a little green because Caleb kissed me softly. "After this is over, we're going back to Grand Marais. We're going to see the sights..."

"The only sight you want to see is me naked underneath you," I teased.

Caleb inclined his head. "Okay, fair, true."

I freed one of my hands and caressed his cheek. "I hope this helps you sleep better at night."

"Yeah, me, too," Caleb said.

Minutes passed. Then hours.

Caleb finally looked down at me, his eyebrows drawn together in the setting sunlight. "I think there might be a problem."

"Let's go back to the boat," I agreed.

We grabbed our life jackets and made our way to the rocky shoreline again.

There, staring up at us with sightless eyes, were the Mounties, laid side-by-side with bullets in their heads.

I stifled a scream as Caleb grabbed me and forced my face into his shoulder so I couldn't see anymore.

I did hear a motor, though, and then a familiar tsking sound.

"You two don't learn, do you," Girard said.

I wrenched my face away from Caleb's shoulder so I could see the leader of the illegal loggers, standing at the front of the boat we'd come in on. The conservation officer was still at the motor. He gave us a wink.

"You... killed two officers of the law..." Caleb stated, gesturing to the bodies on the ground.

"We sure did. And they'll be going in that little cabin, too," Girard replied. "Boy, you've got a lot of blood on your hands."

Oh, the hell with that. "Caleb didn't shoot these men. You've got a lot of blood on YOUR hands!" I protested.

"There's Jacey. Not a wilting flower." Girard grinned at me. "Now, unless you want to end up like these two here, I'd suggest you get in the boat."

"How do we know you won't kill us anyway?" Caleb asked.

Girard snorted. "You don't. But if you stay on that shoreline, it's a guarantee."

Caleb stood, holding me for a long moment. Then Girard leveled a gun on us, and Caleb let me go and took my hand, taking me carefully down over the rocks. He helped me into the boat before getting in himself.

"Good boy," Girard said, putting his gun away. "You two sit tight. We've got a ways to go."

The conservation officer pulled away from the shoreline. Caleb and I sat on the middle seat, while Girard sat down in front, facing us.

"I suppose you had a good reason for bringing two Mounties our way?" Girard asked while the conservation officer got us back to the rocks. We didn't have to ask if we should take up the oars to help get the boat out—we just did it.

"It's my fault," Caleb said quickly. "I couldn't live with what I'd done to Bill. When we went in to report the incident in Grand Marais..."

"Promised you the world, I'm sure," Girard chuckled. "Ah, to be young and stupid again."

"What are you going to do with us?" I whispered.

Girard shrugged. "Haven't decided yet. I do know you won't be telling tales about our operation ever again."

'Oh God,' I thought, pressing closer to Caleb. 'We're going to die.'

ALSO BY M. FRANCIS HASTINGS

Once Bitten
Submitting to My Stepbrother series
Stranded With My Stepbrother
Snatched With My Stepbrother (coming 4/15/2024)

Sign up for my newsletter here: https://subscribepage.io/TfsA3A

Milton Keynes UK
Ingram Content Group UK Ltd.
UKHW051428131024
2153UKWH00019B/86

9 781964 125084